| 35 CENTS

TERRI SCHIAVO CASE

SCHIAVO RECEIVES SACRED RITES

Open for Debate

The Right to Die

The Miami

SATURDAY, MARCH 26, 2005 | 102ND YEAR, NO. 193 | © 2005 THE MIAMI

TERRI SCHIAVO CASE

Plan to seize Schia

...s to Terri Schiavo's protests outside
e hospice grew more fevered.

ERIKA BOLSTAD,
LONG AND CARA BU
dley@herald.com

NELLAS PARK As re...
en Terri Schiavo's family and their sup-
rs Easter Sunday, husband Michael
o made one small but important con-
y gesture: He allowed his dying wife
ve communion.
he Christian calendar's holiest day,
holic priests administered a drop of
ted wine to Schiavo's tongue with an
er and gave her last rites. Her
d sister stood nearby.
chiavo was in her 10th day without
r hydration, and a panicky desper-
aken hold of the people who fer-
ed for her life. Outside the hos-
sioned demonstrators clashed
n the steamy heat, drawing the
e.
t going to solve this problem
g arrested," Schiavo's younger
y Schindler said, as two men
at on-site police. "We can
s. But we're not going to do
etting arrested doesn't help.

STER
rald

AL | ONE DOLLAR

TERRI SCHIAVO CASE

PARENTS' LEGAL BATTLE ENDING

■ The parents' legal battle over Terri S...
virtually ended Saturday as death
nd bitterness persisted.

L LONG, CARA BUC
sherald.com

SCHIAVO RECEIVES SACRED RITES

On Easter Sunday, priests administered Holy Communion and last rites to Terri Schiavo, as protests outside the hospice grew more fevered.

ERIKA BOLSTAD,
[...] LONG AND CARA BUCKLEY
[...]kley@herald.com

[PI]NELLAS PARK — As relations frayed [betw]een Terri Schiavo's family and their sup[porte]rs Easter Sunday, husband Michael [Schiav]o made one small but important con[ciliator]y gesture: He allowed his dying wife [to rece]ive communion.

[On t]he Christian calendar's holiest day, [Cat]holic priests administered a drop of [consecra]ted wine to Schiavo's tongue with an [eyedrop]per and gave her last rites. Her [parents an]d sister stood nearby.

[S]chiavo was in her 10th day without [food o]r hydration, and a panicky desper[ation ha]d taken hold of the people who fer[vently pra]yed for her life. Outside the hos[pice, impa]ssioned demonstrators clashed [...]in the steamy heat, drawing the [polic]e.

[... is no]t going to solve this problem [by bein]g arrested," Schiavo's younger [brother Bobb]y Schindler said, as two men [lunged] at on-site police. "We can [do thi]s. But we're not going to do [it by g]etting arrested doesn't help.

Open for Debate

The Right to Die

by Rebecca Stefoff

Marshall Cavendish
Benchmark
New York

Thanks to Robert Cavalier,
professor of philosophy at Carnegie Mellon University,
for his thoughtful review of the manuscript.

Marshall Cavendish Benchmark
99 White Plains Road
Tarrytown, NY 10591
www.marshallcavendish.us

Copyright © 2009 by Marshall Cavendish Corporation

All rights reserved. No part of this book may be reproduced or utilized in any form
or by any means electronic or mechanical, including photocopying, recording, or by any
information storage and retrieval system, without permission from the copyright holders.

All Web sites were available and accurate when this book was sent to press.

Library of Congress Cataloging-in-Publication Data
Stefoff, Rebecca, [date]
The right to die / by Rebecca Stefoff.
p. cm. — (Open for debate)
Includes bibliographical references and index.
ISBN 978-0-7614-2948-7
1. Right to die—Juvenile literature. 2. Euthanasia—Juvenile literature.
3. Assisted suicide—Juvenile literature. 4. Medical ethics—Juvenile
literature. I. Title.

R726.S675 2009
179.7—dc22

2008000361

Photo research by Lindsay Aveilhe/Linda Sykes Picture Research, Inc., Hilton Head, SC

Cover photo:Jeff Greenberg/Alamy
Jeff Greenberg/Alamy: 6; Courtesy Joni and Friends: 11; © *The Oregonian/* photo
by Bob Finch: 26; The Granger Collection: 31; © Michael Nicholson/Corbis: 47; ©Bettmann/
Corbis: 54; Photo by Ken Ross: 57; AFP/Getty Images: 65; ©Yoav Levy/ Phototake: 71;
AP Photo/Greg Wahl-Stephens: 83; Time and Life Pictures/Getty Images: 87; Jason Reed/
Reuters/Corbis: 89; © Olivier Hoslet/Corbis: 95; © Ed Eckstein/Corbis: 101;
© Michael Mulvey/*Dallas Morning News*/Corbis: 106.

Publisher: Michelle Bisson
Art Director: Anahid Hamparian
Series Designer: Sonia Chaghatzbanian

Printed in Malaysia

1 3 5 6 4 2

Contents

Foreword 7

1 Choices 10

2 Past Perspectives on Suicide and Euthanasia 29

3 The Right to Die Goes Public 52

4 Assisted Suicide and the Law 77

5 For and Against Aid in Dying 99

Notes 109

Further Information 114

Bibliography 117

Index 119

THE POLITICS
OF LIFE AND DEATH:

WHO DECIDES?

State Rep. Dan Gelber, a Democrat from Miami Beach, was one of 24 Florida House members who voted against House Bill 701.

a Republican from

Foreword

Death is universal, which means that when death becomes a social and political issue, it is the one issue that has the power to affect all of us. People may go through life untouched by many of the most controversial topics of the day, such as abortion or same-sex marriage, but no one escapes death.

It is likely that everyone thinks about death at some point. The illness or death of a loved one, perhaps a grandparent or parent, may lead a young person to wonder what his or her own future death will be like. Other people may not consider the question until much later in life, when they feel death draw closer as a result of injury, illness, or simply old age. Today, however, something called "the right to die" is in the news. Headlines are made when family disputes over withdrawing mechanical life support from people in comas erupt into legal and political battles. People rally to support or oppose laws making it legal for physicians to help their patients die under certain circumstances; several countries around the world, as well as one state in the United States, have already passed such laws, and others are under consideration.

The public debate over the right to die sometimes focuses on questions that were once private, or shared only with family and physicians: What if I no longer want to live with incurable illness or unending pain? Would I want to go on living if I lost all control over my life, my dignity, and my body? Other, broader questions are concerned with basic concepts of right and wrong: When is it right to die, or to let someone die? What about *helping* someone die? Finally, there are questions of public policy and law: If individuals claim that they have the right to die, what are society's rights and obligations? Does the state, which has a role in preserving citizens' lives, also have a role in saying when and how people may die? Should euthanasia—killing someone to end his or her suffering—be legalized? How does the law view those who seek to control the time and manner of their own deaths?

These questions are not new. People have pondered them, and sometimes acted on them, for centuries. Yet advances in medicine have changed the way we die, and the ways we think about dying. Modern medicine is one of the great achievements of science and technology. It has defeated many diseases and produced results beyond the dreams of earlier generations of healers. Although medical science can prolong life, sometimes this simply means that it prolongs the process of dying. Some people prefer to let go of life rather than extend it with machines that force their lungs to breathe and with tubes that deliver nourishment into their stomachs. And some believe that they should have the right to use medical science to ease and hasten their deaths, when death is near or life is unbearably painful.

The right to die—often called voluntary euthanasia or assisted suicide—has passionate supporters and equally passionate opponents. They consider whether there is such a thing as a right to die, or an obligation to live; whether people should be allowed to end their own lives with legal approval and medical aid; and what the drawbacks might be if such practices were sanctioned.

Some people approach the issue of the right to die from a religious standpoint. Others view it through the lens of ethics, the branch of philosophy that is concerned with rational inquiry into what is right and what is wrong. Still others speak from legal, medical, or political perspectives. Many people on both sides of the issue speak from deeply felt personal experiences. They have witnessed the lives or deaths of loved ones, or have wrestled with choices about their own fates. Their stories are woven into a debate that is bound to continue as individuals and governments address the complex, controversial question of the right to die.

1
Choices

In the debate over whether it is right for people to hasten their own deaths to end suffering, some of the most eloquent voices are those of people who have faced the question in their own lives or the lives of their loved ones. The range of their choices shows that people's attitudes about death are as individual as the ways in which they lead their lives. Their experiences also suggest that there are no simple, one-size-fits-all answers to questions about how and when life should end.

"This Life's Not Over Yet"

On a hot summer day in 1967, seventeen-year-old Joni Eareckson tried to cool off with what she calls "a reckless dive into some shallow water." She struck the bottom. The impact broke her spine at the base of her neck. Facedown and unconscious, she floated in the water. Her sister saved her from drowning, but the damage to her spinal cord could not be repaired. Eareckson was paralyzed from the neck down.

JONI EARECKSON TADA WANTED TO EXERCISE THE RIGHT TO DIE
AFTER A RECKLESS DIVE LEFT HER SEVERELY DISABLED, BUT IN THE
YEARS SINCE, TADA HAS PLUNGED INTO THE FRAY AS AN ADVOCATE
FOR THE RIGHTS OF THE DISABLED.

The teenager spent a year in the hospital. Her thin body was covered with pressure sores, open wounds that form where flesh and bone rest against a surface without moving for long periods. At times Eareckson had to be force-fed through a tube because she would not eat. She lay wrapped in sheets, "trapped in a canvas cocoon," as she later said. Her head was the only part of her body that she could move; she was now a quadriplegic, someone who has lost the use of all four limbs. She considered herself "little more than a corpse."

Thoughts of death, in fact, were never far from Eareckson's mind during those terrible days. She expressed her despair in a letter she composed in her mind:

To Whom It May Concern:
I hate my life. You can't imagine the ache of wanting to end your life and not being able to because you're a quadriplegic and can't use your hands.

After the doctors did surgery on my neck, I refused to wear a neck collar. I hate it too. Nobody understands and nobody will listen to me when I tell them I don't want to live. People feel sorry for me and I can't stand it. I can't even go to the bathroom by myself.

I don't have the energy to cope, I don't have the strength to face the next day. I want out.

A depressed teenager

As she lay in her hospital bed, Eareckson dreamed of the day when she would be able to sit up in a motorized wheelchair. She planned to drive it off a high curb. Maybe that would end her life. Seeking other avenues to self-destruction, she begged a friend to bring her mother's sleeping pills or her father's razor blades to the hospital; the friend refused. When there were no nurses around,

Eareckson flung her head about on her pillow as hard as she could, hoping to break her neck again, this time fatally.

But Eareckson did not die. As time went on, she found herself enjoying the company of people who spent time at her bedside, telling jokes or sharing homemade cookies. One friend, a young man named Steve, talked with Eareckson about the Bible and the Christian faith. Eareckson's own faith deepened and, she says, "I had found an answer that made life worth living." Eareckson became convinced that her life, with all its burden of suffering, was part of God's plan, and that God would give her the strength not just to endure it but to enjoy it.

Since leaving the hospital in 1968, Eareckson has spent her life in a wheelchair. Yet her disability did not keep her from meeting and marrying Ken Tada, nor did it prevent her from traveling and finding satisfaction in creative outlets. She taught herself to paint, holding a brush in her mouth, and she also began writing. In addition to telling her own story of faith triumphing over despair, she has written books about the lives of the disabled and the challenges they face in society.

Joni Eareckson Tada became a well-known advocate for the disabled, someone who calls for greater understanding of disabled people's needs as well as more resources, such as counseling and suitable homes, to meet those needs. Religious faith has remained a cornerstone of her life. She founded Joni and Friends, a nonprofit organization that works to help Christian churches expand their services and ministry to the disabled.

In her 1992 book *When Is It Right to Die?*, Tada tackled the topics of suicide and euthanasia, or killing someone to end suffering. The situations she describes in the book fall into two broad categories. One category includes people who are permanently disabled or incurably ill—people whose lives may be difficult and painful, but who are still able to go on living. The other contains people who are in the final stages of illness or in a coma and are being kept alive by various forms of life support. For those in the second category, Tada says, the decision about whether to "pull the plug" and let yourself or a loved one die must be a personal one, shaped by the circumstances of the individual and family involved. Tada argues, however, that people in the first category should never give in to despair or depression. In her view, thoughts of ending life or hastening death to escape suffering are temptations sent by the devil. The right course is to trust God and live. "Be patient," she writes. "Don't give up. This life's not over yet. It will get better."

Joni Eareckson Tada's story raises a number of issues that are extremely important in any discussion of the right to die. One issue is competence. In legal and medical contexts, someone is considered competent, or capable of making major decisions, only if he or she has full understanding and powers of reason. Minors are not competent to make their own decisions because their powers of understanding have not yet matured; people whose judgment is impaired by mental illness or mental disability are also not considered competent. In such cases parents and guardians make the necessary health-care decisions.

At the time of her injury, Tada was a minor. She lacked the legal right to make decisions affecting her care. Even if her right to die had been recognized by law in the late 1960s—which it was not—her requests to die would not have been honored because she was a minor and, therefore, not legally competent to make such a decision. Later Tada was deeply grateful that no one had responded to her pleas for death, and she now opposes voluntary euthanasia. Even the strongest supporters of the right to die, however, acknowledge that only competent adults should exercise such a right.

Another concern that underlies many debates about euthanasia and the right to die is the difference among patients' conditions. Tada raises this issue when she talks about different types of suffering: being a quadriplegic in a wheelchair, for example, in contrast to being in a coma with no functional brain activity, or being in the final stages of an incurable illness such as cancer. If it becomes easy for people to pull the plug on family members who are being kept alive by machines in hospitals, if society allows people who are nearing death to hasten their own ends, will it also become easier for someone in a wheelchair to choose death because that person considers life no longer worth living, even though many people in the same situation feel very differently about their lives? Could the right-to-die movement reach beyond those who are dying to affect those who are merely disabled? Should it? These questions are of deep concern to many disabled people and others who hope to influence the public debate about euthanasia.

Finally, Tada's story introduces another important part of the right-to-die debate: religion. Her testimony about the need to choose life over death is rooted in her own heartfelt Christian faith. Tada found peace and acceptance through God, and clearly, she hopes that others will do so, too. She is not alone. Many people who oppose assisted suicide or voluntary euthanasia do so out of religious conviction. They feel that choosing death, even to escape great suffering, is against God's will. Yet other Christians, religious leaders and scholars among them, support the individual's right to die, at least in certain circumstances. And what about people of different beliefs, and people who are nonbelievers? Supporters of voluntary euthanasia claim that while believers have every right to follow their beliefs, those beliefs should not limit the choices of people who do not share them.

"It's an Issue of Individual Rights"

At first glance Dax Cowart may seem to be an unlikely spokesman for the right to die. Cowart lived through a horrific accident and the agonizing medical treatments that followed, then went on to attend law school, marry, and become a successful attorney and public speaker. He is a survivor. Yet he argues passionately for the right of the severely injured to die if they wish to do so—a right that was withheld from him.

Cowart was twenty-five years old in 1973. After leaving the air force, he was working in his father's real-estate business in Texas. One day he and his father drove into the countryside to look at a piece of land that was for sale. They had no way of knowing that a leak in an underground pipeline had filled the area with odorless propane gas. When the Cowarts had finished looking at the property and were ready to leave, they tried to start their car. This caused the gas to explode in a fireball that, Cowart later learned, scorched an area almost a mile long.

After running through three walls of fire, Cowart rolled on the ground to put out the flames that were devouring his clothes, then ran down the road screaming for help. A man ran up and helped Cowart lie down on the grass while a boy ran to summon an ambulance. Most of Cowart's clothing had been burned off, along with much of his skin. He had third-degree burns over two-thirds of his body; his eyes, ears, and hands were destroyed by the fire. "The burns were unbearable," Cowart recalled in a 1991 interview. "I never knew that kind of pain could even exist." As he lay there in agony, Cowart asked the man to bring him a gun, saying, "I've got to let myself out of this misery." In what Cowart remembers as "a very kind and caring way," the man replied, "I can't do that."

Cowart's father, also horribly burned, died in the ambulance that carried the two men to the hospital. Cowart wished many times that he had shared his father's fate. In the days and weeks that followed, as he endured extreme pain and underwent the even more painful treatments necessary to remove dead and infected tissue from burn victims, Cowart asked many times to be allowed to die. "All I wanted to do was end it," he says, looking back. "I was telling the doctors that from the very beginning."

He kept telling them that, for months. All of his requests were ignored. Cowart's doctors, overriding Cowart's own repeated wishes, carried out what he calls an aggressive treatment plan aimed at saving his life at any cost. The doctors' reasoning infuriated Cowart. When he told them that he would rather die than continue to live in agony, they decided that he was in too much pain to be competent to make the decision. When they gave him medication for the pain, they declared that the drugs made him incompetent to make the decision—but they never gave him enough medication to truly control his pain because they feared creating a drug addiction.

After what he calls "unbearable pain that I went through for many, many months," Cowart was pronounced "healed." Blind, scarred, and helpless in many ways, he endured pain and depression for years afterward. A lawsuit against the company that owned the leaky pipeline made him financially secure, and eventually law school and the practice of law gave him a purpose. He declared in 1991, "I feel that I have a very good quality of life and I enjoy life." He added, however, that he had paid an unimaginably high price in pain for his survival. Cowart still firmly believed that his doctors should have respected his wishes and allowed him to refuse treatment. "I had no idea," he has said, "that in the United States of America a mentally competent adult could be forcibly treated or forced to stay in a hospital."

Cowart feels that severely ill or injured people should

be allowed to end their lives. Individuals' rights to control their own health care, he believes, are fundamental:

> Once the patient has been given the information necessary to make a truly informed choice, then the patient's choice should be respected. When it comes to a mentally competent adult, no one has the right to force their will upon another human being. The right to control our own body is a right that we are born with. It's not something that we have to ask anyone else for, not the treating physician, not the government and not our next of kin. There can never be a legitimate law that takes away an individual's right to control their own body. . . . There is no legitimate authority for saying, "I don't care what you think or how you feel about it, I know better."

Cowart is pleased that in the years since his accident, the courts have upheld the right of the individual to refuse unwanted medical treatment. If his accident happened today, he believes, he would have a better chance of having his decision respected, and being allowed to die without treatment. Cowart also feels that more active ways of helping patients die, such as assisted suicide, should be legalized. The laws governing assisted suicide, however, should require patients to have access to counseling and full information about all their possible choices. If, after counseling, a patient decides to end his or her life, "then that individual should be given assistance in dying," Cowart says.

Dax Cowart's views about the right to die are based on a strong sense of personal autonomy, or self-determination. Autonomy grants a person the freedom to make the decisions that shape his or her own life. Cowart's position is shared by many people who place a high value on independence, autonomy, and individualism—qualities that Europeans and Americans have increasingly prized for the past few centuries. This position may be summed up as "I should be allowed to do what I want, as long as my actions harm no one else."

Another point of view, however, is that each person is part of society, and that social values are the sum of everyone's individual actions. People who focus on this view might believe that an individual's decision to end life or hasten death *does* harm others. It weakens society by ignoring or denying the interconnections that exist among people, whether in families, communities, hospitals and nursing homes, workplaces, or the larger civic body. When it comes to forming policies or writing laws that address the right to die, a core question concerns how best to balance individual and social values.

"Dying in the Modern World"

Journalist Sue Woodman was writing a book about the controversy over the right to die when she found herself watching her beloved aunt struggle with difficult end-of-life decisions. Aunty, as Woodman's ninety-year-old aunt was called, broke her leg in a fall. Surgery was needed to repair the leg, but the operation would be risky. Plagued with heart disease, diabetes, and high blood pressure, Aunty might die during surgery. She understood the risks and had agreed to the operation.

Woodman, Aunty's closest living relative, traveled to London to be at Aunty's side. She expected that either Aunty would survive the operation and soon be out of danger, or she would die. "I had no idea," Woodman wrote in her 1998 book *Last Rights: The Struggle Over the Right to Die*, "that there might be another, even worse, outcome to the scenario."

Aunty lived through the operation. The doctors discovered, however, that a blood clot was preventing blood from reaching her lower leg. At this point Aunty had just two choices: an amputation of the leg above the knee, or death from gangrene, probably within a week.

Woodman asked Aunty if she was afraid to die, and Aunty declared that she was not. She said, "I would love it—just to go to sleep, to be finished. . . ." Such an outcome was possible. The nurses had already given Aunty morphine to keep her from feeling pain for what remained of her life if she decided against the amputation. Yet when a doctor told Aunty that her chances of surviving the amputation were fifty-fifty, perhaps even a little better, she chose to have a second operation, this one to remove most of her leg.

Again Aunty survived the surgery. Afterward she was depressed and full of new fears. What would her life be like now? Would she be able to go home, or would she have to move into a care institution? Still, as Woodman sat beside Aunty's bed, Aunty suddenly said, out of the blue, "I think I made the right choice." Woodman wondered what was going through Aunty's mind: "Was it, perhaps, the sun streaming in through the windows, or an instant free of pain, a minuscule surge of well-being, that persuaded her, at least for that moment, that it was worth being alive?"

Aunty never did go home. She left the hospital for a rehabilitation center, and she left the center for a nursing home. There was space for very few of her own possessions in her small room. Although Aunty tried to learn to walk with a prosthetic leg, she could not manage it. The rest of her life was spent in a wheelchair. Aunty felt humiliation and outrage when she had to ask for help in matters such as going to the bathroom. She spent a lot of time in her room, for she took no pleasure in the company of the other residents of the home—she called them "the shriekers and the shakers." Her moods swung from depression to anger. She told people that she wanted to die. She told Woodman that she wanted "death to come like a thunderbolt, to take her, quickly and painlessly, for life suddenly to stop."

Very few people are fortunate enough to die like that. Aunty was not one of them. She grew weaker, and eventually she developed a serious chest infection. After several days in the hospital, with two tubes carrying oxygen into her lungs and a third dripping pain medication into her arm, she gasped and died. "In the end," Woodman wrote, "it looked so easy. But the suffering Aunty endured through her final traumatic 18 months haunts me still. . . . She told me that if she had known what her life would be like after the amputation, she would never have gone through with it."

Woodman wondered, however, whether Aunty could truly have imagined what her life would become. At the time that Aunty had to make her vital decisions, she still had hope that some recognizable form of her life—a life with known limits, but also a life with some pleasure and autonomy—would go on. Woodman also wondered whether Aunty would have chosen the option of a quiet, painless death under medical supervision if physician-assisted suicide had been legal. Woodman will never know, but Aunty's ordeal, like other deaths Woodman chronicled for her book, showed her that "dying in the modern world is often hard . . . a journey taken without adequate guides."

Aunty's story also reveals how difficult it is to know how someone else truly feels about the choice between living and dying. Before her first operation, Aunty seemed to want her life to be over, yet she chose to undergo surgery twice in the hope that life would go on. People's hopes and

Language for the End of Life

The debate over the right to die includes a vocabulary of special terms. Some of these terms are medical, some are legal, and some come from the activists who oppose an individual's right to die, or those who support it. The meanings of these terms often overlap; in addition, different organizations or individuals may use the same term in different ways.

advance directives: Legal documents prepared by adults who are competent (capable of understanding the outcomes of various courses of action, and of making informed decisions) that spell out the health-care decisions they want made for them if they become unable to make such decisions in the future. The three most common types of advance directive are the **DNR order**, the **living will**, and the **durable power of attorney for health care**.

ANH: Artificial nutrition and hydration, the medical practice of administering nourishment through tubes to patients who cannot eat or drink; one form of life support.

DNR order: "Do Not Resuscitate," a medical order that means that no medical action should be taken to revive the patient if his or her breathing or heartbeat stops; the order must be requested by a competent adult and signed by a physician.

double effect: An action that has two clearly foreseen effects, or outcomes. One outcome is desirable and intended; the other is undesirable, but not intended. In end-of-life situations the double effect usually refers to physicians giving terminally ill patients high doses of medication to relieve pain. The physician knows that the medications may also hasten death but does not prescribe them for that reason.

durable power of attorney for health care: A type of **advance directive** in which a competent adult names someone as a proxy who will make health-care decisions for the person in case he or she is unable to make those decisions; the proxy does not have to be a family member; usually seen by hospitals and courts as a stronger form of advance directive than a **living will**.

euthanasia: Ending the life of someone who is suffering or is incurably or **terminally ill**, based solely on the wishes of the person affected. Passive euthanasia means letting someone die by withholding potentially life-prolonging medical care or by ending medical intervention, such as a feeding tube, that is keeping the person alive. Active euthanasia means doing something to end the person's life, such as giving a lethal injection. Voluntary euthanasia is killing or letting die someone who has requested death as an alternative to suffering. Non-voluntary euthanasia is doing the same thing, but to someone who is unconscious or unable to give consent, except through an advance directive. Involuntary euthanasia is killing or letting die someone against his or her wishes—in other words, murder.

hospice: An organization or setting that offers care and aid to people who are **terminally ill**, and often to their families as well.

living will: The first type of **advance directive** used in the United States; a document in which a competent adult specifies the types of medical treatments that should be given or withheld if he or she becomes incompetent and cannot control his or her own treatment; usually seen as a protection against unwanted measures to prolong life through artificial means (life-support mechanisms).

palliative care: Medical or **hospice** treatment to improve the comfort of people who are incurably ill or dying; may include things such as pain medication and counseling, but is not intended to cure an illness or condition; sometimes called comfort care.

physician-assisted suicide: Suicide by an incurably or terminally ill person who uses a means of death, such as a lethal injection or dose of medication, that was provided by a physician for the specific purpose of causing the patient's death; the physician, however, does not administer the fatal treatment. Sometimes called physician aid-in-dying or hastened death.

terminally ill: In the final and fatal stage of an illness or disorder. Many medical and **hospice** organizations consider a patient terminally ill if he or she is expected to die within six months.

fears shift constantly, and their desires do not always come into clear view, even to themselves. It is not surprising that many people are reluctant to decide which end-of-life conditions they would find intolerable, or that they hesitate to spell out exactly what decisions they would make for themselves in a crisis, or would want others to make for them if need be.

"I'm Really Ready to Go"

Lovelle Svart did not flinch from confronting the details of her death. She planned the day, the time, and the manner of it, right down to the party. Svart, who lived in Portland, Oregon, was a longtime smoker. In her late fifties she learned that she had lung cancer. Although medical treatment slowed the growth and spread of the cancer, doctors were unable to destroy the cancer or remove it. A few years later Svart underwent open-heart surgery. The operation kept her heart going—but the cancer was still going, too.

By June 2007 Svart had been living with cancer for five years. At that point her doctor told her that she had entered the terminal phase of her illness and was likely to die within six months. As she faced her coming death, Svart was aware that she had an option that is available to Americans only in the state of Oregon. Under a law called the Oregon Death with Dignity Act (DWDA), first approved by voters and the state legislature in 1994, a person who is terminally ill may request medical help in ending his or her life. After Svart chose to exercise that right, her doctor wrote a prescription for a lethal dose of medication.

Svart had the prescription filled on August 7. She was not sure, she said, whether or not she would use it, but it comforted her "to know it was there." Before long, however, Svart's symptoms became more difficult to bear. She experienced shortness of breath and nausea in addition to

LOVELLE SVART (*LEFT*) CHOSE TO CELEBRATE HER RIGHT TO DIE WITH A GOODBYE PARTY FOR HERSELF. SHE WENT OUT LAUGHING.

pain. Tumors growing in her throat made it increasingly hard for her to swallow. Rather than allowing her worsening symptoms to rob her of all control, Svart decided to die while she was still able to swallow the prescription. She also decided that she would share the day of her death with loved ones, friends, and supporters, who were invited to join her at her mother's apartment for the event.

On the chosen day Svart attached a note to her mother's door: "Please Do NOT Disturb. Unless Urgent. Thank you." She ordered platters of sandwiches and fruit from a store, decorated the table with pink roses, and set up a machine to play her favorite music: polkas. She also discovered that her car battery had died and arranged to have the battery charged. Later, when a friend asked why

Svart had spent part of her last day alive worrying about a car battery, Svart said, "The car goes to my sister. I didn't want it to be dead."

People close to Svart, including her mother and three siblings, gathered for an afternoon of stories, jokes, and conversations. At one point Svart danced a polka with George Eighmey, the director of an organization called Compassion & Choices of Oregon, which helps some of the people who hasten their deaths under the DWDA's provisions.

"I feel so at peace," Svart declared. "I've had such a good time. . . . I'm really ready to go." Everyone lined up to hug Svart and say farewell, some laughing, some crying. Then, after a trip outside for a last cigarette, Svart went into the bedroom, lay down, and prepared to die. She had already taken several pills to control nausea and prevent her from vomiting after she drank the lethal dose.

Eighmey now asked her, "Is this what you really want?" and reminded her that if she drank the dose, she would die. Svart reaffirmed that she understood, and that it was what she wanted. She then drank the dose. As her mother lay next to her on the bed, Svart said, "I'm fine, Mom." A moment later she said, "I'm peaceful. It stopped raining, the sun's out. And I've had a wonderful day." Then: "It's starting to hit me now." Svart fell asleep, drifted into a coma, and died five hours later, peacefully and without regaining consciousness.

Throughout the last three months of her life, Svart maintained an online video diary that she called "Living to the End." She talked about the pleasures and pains of life as she moved toward her death, and she shared her thoughts and feelings about her decision to die with dignity. Svart hoped that her online diary would encourage people to think and talk about death more openly and less fearfully. Among the thousands of people who commented on Svart's diary were many who thanked her for helping them start difficult conversations. One woman wrote that Svart's diary had enabled her to talk "in a new way" to her young teenagers about both smoking and death. Others said that Svart had given them the courage to communicate with friends who were dying.

The Internet allowed Lovelle Svart to share her progress toward death with people around the world. A generation ago such a thing would have been unimaginable. Medical science and technology, however, have transformed death much more profoundly. Doctors can now keep people alive in many circumstances that formerly would have been fatal. As a result the conditions of death in the modern world are relatively new in human history. Yet people have been thinking and talking about dying— and debating the question of whether it is right to seek one's own death—for a long, long time.

2

Past Perspectives on Suicide and Euthanasia

Today's debate over the right to die focuses on physician-assisted suicide and voluntary euthanasia. These terms describe situations in which a person chooses death as the alternative to a terminal or incurable illness, or to unbearable pain, and requests help in dying. Physician-assisted suicide and voluntary euthanasia, however, cannot easily be detached from their larger frameworks: suicide and euthanasia.

Suicide has had many meanings over the centuries. In some cultures and in some circumstances, it has been regarded as honorable. Many views of suicide in Western societies, however, have been negative; the desire to end one's life has been considered a form of cowardice, a sin, or a mental disorder. Euthanasia, too, is a term with a history. It has been used as a label for "mercy killings," but there have been times when it was used to get rid of "weaklings" or the "unfit." The current debate about the right to die is colored by these facts. Although the controversy over right-to-die laws may be a recent social and political development, it is inescapably related to the long history of thought about death and the taking of life.

Suicide in the Ancient World

The ancient Greeks, Romans, and Jews held a wide variety of views about suicide. Among the Greeks, for example, laws about suicide varied from one city-state to another. In some city-states, including Athens, Sparta, and Thebes, the law dictated that the bodies of people who had committed suicide should be punished, although it is not clear how consistently that law was carried out. The spirits of those who had killed themselves, it was thought, were especially restless and could trouble the living. Athenian law said that the right hand of a suicide should be cut off to prevent the spirit from committing crimes. Other societies have also mutilated the corpses of suicides in various ways, either for protection from the supposed spirits of the dead or as punishment for the crime of suicide.

The people of ancient Athens may have punished the corpses of those who killed themselves, but according to a Greek scholar named Libanius they also legalized suicide. Libanius, who lived in the fourth century CE, wrote that in earlier ages, Athenian law had allowed people to request state aid in ending their lives through the use of a poison known as hemlock:

> **Whoever no longer wishes to live shall state his reasons to the Senate, and after having received permission shall abandon life. If your existence is hateful to you, die; if you are overwhelmed by fate, drink the hemlock. If you are bowed with grief, abandon life. Let the unhappy man recount his misfortune, let the magistrate [administrator of laws] supply him with the remedy, and his wretchedness will come to an end.**

The process described by Libanius sounds a bit like the forms of assisted suicide that have become legal in a few places in the twenty-first century, except that today physicians, not magistrates, provide permission and aid in dying, and the reasons for seeking death are supposed to be strictly medical.

Hemlock was the lethal agent in the most famous suicide of the ancient Greek world—the death of the philosopher Socrates in 399 BCE. The magistrates of Athens, convinced that Socrates's teachings were having a dangerous effect on the young men of the city, ordered the philosopher to poison himself. Some regard his death as a suicide rather than an execution because he could have fled the city but chose to drink the hemlock, as ordered.

Greek history, legend, and mythology contain many

THE QUESTION OF WHETHER SOCRATES DRANK THE HEMLOCK AS AN ACT OF SUICIDE OR OF STATE-SANCTIONED MURDER WILL NEVER BE SOLVED, BUT WILL ALWAYS BE PICTURED. THIS 1787 PAINTING BY FRENCH PAINTER JACQUES LOUIS DAVID IS JUST ONE OF THE MANY ARTISTIC RENDERINGS OF THE DEATH OF SOCRATES.

other stories about people who killed themselves for a variety of reasons: out of remorse for something bad they had done; to avoid bringing dishonor to their families or cities; to escape rape or seduction; out of grief at the loss of a loved one; or to escape the ravages of old age, illness, and dependency. These characters are usually portrayed with admiration, or at least as honorable figures, which indicates that most Greeks did not regard suicide as an absolute wrong.

The Pythagoreans were an exception. This school of religious and philosophical thinkers, followers of the philosopher and mathematician Pythagoras, considered suicide wrong under any circumstances. They believed that the gods sent souls into earthly bodies as a form of discipline, and that it was an offense to the gods to end one's life prematurely. Yet some ancient sources say that Pythagoras himself committed suicide, either by starving himself to death or by letting enemies capture him when he refused to walk across a field of beans, which the Pythagoreans regarded as sacred.

Other schools of philosophy held more tolerant, even positive, views of suicide. The Epicureans, who argued that the purpose of life was enjoyment, claimed that it was reasonable to withdraw from a life that had ceased to offer pleasure and had become intolerable. The Stoics believed that life should be governed by reason, not by passion, pleasure, or pain. People should live in a dignified manner, in harmony with nature. Death was not terrifying—it was simply a choice to be made rationally. The third-century scholar Diogenes Laertius, who wrote a history of philosophy, summed up the Stoics' view of suicide: "The wise man can with reason give his life for his country and his friends, or he can kill himself if he suffers serious pain, if he has lost a limb, or if he has an incurable illness."

The Greek thinkers who had the deepest and most

lasting effect on Western thought were Socrates's student Plato and Plato's student Aristotle. Each of them addressed the subject of suicide. Plato's views are complex and sometimes contradictory. In a work called the *Republic*, Plato compares suicide to the wrongful act of a soldier on duty who leaves his post without permission. In the *Laws*, he says that those who end their own lives cheat fate, and that they should be buried without honor—yet he also says that suicide can be honorable if it is ordered by the state, or if a person chooses suicide as an alternative to terrible misfortune or disgrace. In the *Phaedo*, which tells of the death of Socrates, Plato appears to present Socrates's own views. Because people belong to the gods, Socrates says, the act of suicide is disrespectful to the gods. Yet Socrates goes on to describe death as highly desirable—what reasonable person would not want to leave the imperfect world to dwell in an ideal state?

Aristotle's views on suicide are far more straightforward than Plato's. Suicide, Aristotle writes in a work called the *Ethics*, is wrong. It is a cowardly avoidance of the individual's duty to the city. When faced with even the worst misfortunes, a virtuous person endures with strength and calmness rather than seeking to escape through death.

Acceptance of suicide may have reached its height in ancient Rome, where many elite, well-educated people were influenced by the philosophy of the Stoics. Rome had no laws or religious rules against suicide. A person's life was considered his or her own, to end at will, and whether a particular suicide was regarded as good or bad depended on the reason for it. In general the Romans thought especially highly of wives who killed themselves after their husbands died, women who killed themselves after being raped, and men who killed themselves to avoid a dishonorable punishment or to escape from the physical weakness of old age. Such approval, however, did not extend to all classes of society. Suicide was the privilege of aristocrats and free citizens. Slaves and soldiers, whose lives had economic value to their masters and to the state, were forbidden to kill themselves and were punished if they tried. Like ancient Greece, Rome had its share of philosophical suicides, people (usually men) who killed themselves in keeping with their ideas. Nothing threatened the life of the orator Cato when he killed himself, so his suicide was seen as a statement of pure liberty and autonomy—a man creating his own fate. Others, such as the poet Lucretius, killed themselves out of pessimism or a feeling expressed in Latin as *taedium vitae*, a weary distaste for life. The Roman writer Seneca, who considered himself a Stoic, described that feeling in the first century CE:

We lack the strength to bear anything: work, pleasure, ourselves, everything in the world is a burden to us. There are some whom this leads to suicide because their perpetual variations make them turn forever in the same circle and because they have made all novelty impossible for themselves; they lose their taste for life and the universe and feel rising up in themselves the cry of hearts made rotten by pleasure: "What? Always the same thing?"

Like other Romans, Seneca felt that it was proper to choose the time and manner of one's death under some circumstances. For an old or sick person to commit suicide solely to escape mere pain was weak and cowardly. Suicide to escape helplessness and the loss of one's mind, however, was rational. He wrote:

Old age, if it lasts very long, brings few to death unmarred: for many of the aged life collapses into

34

lethargy and impotence. After that do you consider a scrap of life a more poignant loss than the freedom to end it? . . . I shan't cast old age off if old age keeps me whole for myself—whole, I mean, on my better side; but if it begins to unseat my reason and pull it piecemeal, if it leaves me not life but mere animation, I shall be out of my crumbling, tumble-down tenement at a bound.

At about the age of seventy, Seneca committed suicide, but not because he was bored with life or losing his reason. Accused of plotting to kill a former pupil, the emperor Nero, Seneca took his own life rather than be executed.

Unlike the Greeks and Romans, the Jews condemned suicide in nearly all circumstances. According to their shared religious beliefs, suicide, or self-murder, was a sin against God, the giver and taker of life. It was an arrogant act that defied God's will.

Jewish religious tradition also addressed the question of euthanasia. In considering whether it is right to hasten death in order to relieve suffering, a medieval Jewish document called the *Sefer Hasidim* declares that neither euthanasia nor suicide is permissible: "If a person is suffering from extreme pain and he says to another: 'You see that I shall not live; kill me because I cannot bear the pain,' one is forbidden to touch him. . . . If a person is suffering great pain and knows that he will not live, he cannot kill himself."

One type of suicide was permitted under Jewish law— a special kind of suicide called martyrdom, in which a person voluntarily accepts death, or sacrifices his or her life, for the sake of a religious belief or principle. Someone who allows himself to be put to death rather than deny his faith, for example, is a martyr.

The most revered example of martyrdom in Jewish tradition took place at a fortress called Masada in 73 CE. According to an account written at the time by a historian named Josephus, Jewish rebels involved in an uprising against Roman rule seized the fortress. Roman forces besieged it, but when the Romans finally entered Masada, they found that more than 900 men, women, and children had killed themselves rather than fall into the enemy's hands. Some archaeologists and historians have questioned this version of events; still, Jews and others hold the mass suicide at Masada in high honor as an example of self-sacrifice by people who put loyalty to their faith and their cause above personal survival.

The Christian View Takes Hold

Martyrdom was also respected in the Christian faith, which by the fourth century CE was well on its way to becoming the dominant religion of the Western world. Christians viewed Jesus Christ, the founder of their faith, as a martyr, because his death could be understood as a voluntary self-sacrifice. So inspiring was his example during the first few centuries of Christianity that leading thinkers of the church worried that there were too many willing martyrs.

One of the most influential early Christian thinkers was Augustine of Hippo. Active in the late fourth and early fifth centuries, Augustine later became a saint of the Roman Catholic Church. In his book *The City of God*, Augustine states clearly that suicide is wrong. It is an act of self-murder, forbidden by the biblical commandment that says: Thou shalt not kill. Even the act of taking one's own life to escape violence or sin—sometimes regarded as heroic martyrdom by early Christians—is forbidden, because it is wrong to substitute one evil act, self-murder, for another evil act. Only if God directly commands it may a human being commit suicide without sinning.

Like Augustine, Thomas Aquinas became a Roman Catholic saint. Aquinas, the foremost Christian thinker of the Middle Ages, lived during the thirteenth century—the dawn of the Renaissance, when Europeans were beginning to rediscover the writings of the ancient Greeks and Romans. Aquinas's writings draw upon the work of earlier Christian scholars, but they also show the strong influence of Aristotle.

Aquinas's position on suicide is similar to Augustine's: Self-murder is forbidden unless ordered by God. Yet Aquinas gives other reasons why suicide is wrong. Like Aristotle, who considered individuals in their role as members of a political community, Aquinas says that suicide is wrong because it breaks the bond between people and society—someone who commits suicide is acting as though he or she exists alone. In another argument that echoes Aristotle, Aquinas claims that suicide is a violation of natural law, because it is the nature of all living things to want to continue living. Finally Aquinas agrees with other Christian thinkers that suicide is a sin because it is an attempt by a human being to seize God's power over life and death.

The idea that individuals might have a right to die was completely outside the mainstream of Christian thought. Throughout the Middle Ages both public opinion and religious teaching were against suicide. The most widely held belief was that acts or thoughts of self-destruction were inspired by the devil.

By the fourteenth century, intolerance of suicide had hardened into a body of church and civil laws that made suicide both a sin and a crime. The only excuse for suicide was insanity. Although the term *euthanasia* was not used during the Middle Ages, killing someone else to end his or her pain was no better than suicide. It was regarded as murder, which was equally sinful and criminal.

A Right to Die in Utopia?

Voluntary death and aid in dying appeared in a 1515 book called *Utopia*, by Thomas More, an English thinker and writer. Although More discussed what today would be called the right to die, scholars disagree on how to interpret his words.

More coined the name *Utopia* from Greek words meaning "no place." Utopia was an imaginary land, the setting of what More described as an ideal society. Later, as other writers proceeded to create their own visions of perfect civilizations, the term *utopia* came to refer to any fictional society that was organized to provide an ideal life for its citizens (of course, the definition of the "ideal life" varied widely). In time an opposite term, *dystopia*, came into use as a label for a fictional account of the worst imaginable society.

Even in More's perfect world, pain and illness were present. He explained how the citizens of Utopia dealt with those problems:

If a disease is not only incurable but also distressing and agonizing without any cessation, then the priests and the public officials exhort [urge] the man, since he is now unequal to all life's duties, a burden to himself, and a trouble to others, and is living beyond the time of his death, to make up his mind not to foster the pest or plague any longer nor to hesitate to die now that life is

torture to him but, relying on good hope, to free himself from this bitter life as from prison and the rack, or else voluntarily to permit others to free him. In this course he will act wisely since by death he will put an end not to enjoyment but to torture.

More, a devout Catholic who was later made a saint, spoke out strongly against suicide in another work called *A Dialogue of Comfort Against Tribulation.* He also refused to consider suicide as an avenue of escape for himself when he was imprisoned in the Tower of London, awaiting execution by beheading for his religious opposition to the king. So how seriously should we take More's calm, reasonable presentation of euthanasia in *Utopia*?

Not too seriously, say some scholars. Michael M. Uhlmann, editor of a 1998 book on the right-to-die debate, points out that *Utopia* can be read as "a highly ironic, satirical work," meaning that it is full of mockery, deliberate exaggeration, and criticism disguised as praise. On the other hand, More once quoted a line from the ancient poet Horace, who said that a person can speak the truth when jesting. Many scholars have suggested that More used the gimmick of an imaginary land—at least in part—as a tool for serious exploration of controversial topics.

Georges Minois, author of a history of suicide in Western thought, points out that More set "strict limits to the right to die" in *Utopia*. If a Utopian committed suicide without social sanctions—in other words, without the permission of the priests and the government—the body was cast without honor into a marsh. Yet those who committed suicide with society's approval, in order to escape terrible illness, were buried with honor. This leads Minois to think that More saw a genuine distinction between wrongful and rightful suicides. "The Utopians practice euthanasia," Minois concludes, "and there is no reason to believe that More was not speaking seriously when he treats the topic."

Except in cases of obvious insanity, suicide brought harsh legal penalties. Some of these penalties were visited upon the suicide's corpse. A thirteenth-century law from the French town of Lille, for example, stated that a male suicide's corpse was to be hanged and a female's burned. In the Swiss city of Zurich, suicides' remains were punished in a way tailored to the manner of death. Wooden stakes were driven into the skulls of those who had stabbed themselves, while those who had drowned themselves were buried at the water's edge. At the very least the body of a suicide was denied burial in the sacred grounds of a cemetery.

Antisuicide laws also targeted the families of people who killed themselves. Laws in many places gave some or all of a suicide's property to the king or the government, not to the dead person's family or heirs. In some parts of Europe, houses and farms that had belonged to suicides were destroyed. Eventually, however, society began to think that it was unfair to punish people simply because they were unlucky enough to be related to a suicide. Most of the laws that caused suicides' property to be confiscated or destroyed had been repealed by the beginning of the nineteenth century. By that time European thinkers and physicians had been reconsidering suicide itself for several centuries.

Enlightened Ideas

As early as the sixteenth century some European intellectuals were beginning to think and write about suicide and euthanasia in new ways. In France, Michel de Montaigne wrote an essay in which he summarized statements in favor of voluntary death from ancient writers, then reviewed Christian arguments against suicide. Montaigne concluded that the question of suicide can be answered only by individual decisions, not by abstract rules. He cautions against hasty or reckless decisions: "Not all troubles are worth our wanting to die to avoid them. And then, there being so many sudden changes in human affairs, it is hard to judge just at what point we are at the end of our hope." Yet when the choice is between voluntary death and the agony of torture or of endless, painful illness, Montaigne does not condemn suicide. "Unendurable pain and fear of a worse death," he says, "seem the most excusable motives for suicide."

In the early seventeenth century John Donne, an English poet, clergyman, and lawyer, wrote *Biathanatos*, a book about suicide; he shared the book with friends but did not allow it to be published during his lifetime. Although Donne revealed that he often thought about suicide, *Biathanatos* is an abstract work, not a personal one.

Donne offers counterarguments to the traditional Aristotelian and Christian arguments against suicide. He claims that a desire to end one's life is not always a violation of natural law, that it does not always harm the community, and that the Bible does not condemn all suicides as immoral. Like Montaigne, Donne concludes that whether suicide is right or wrong depends on the motives in each case. Suicide may have moral Christian motives, such as martyrdom or preserving the welfare of other people. *Biathanatos*, however, does not say that people have a right to die, or to help others die, to escape suffering.

The eighteenth century brought to Europe an intellectual and cultural movement known as the Enlightenment. Inspired by the idea that human life should be ordered by reason rather than tradition, some philosophers, political scientists, and writers turned a critical eye on established institutions, including government and religion. A number of Enlightenment philosophers published their thoughts on suicide. David Hume of Scotland, Voltaire of France, and Immanuel Kant of Germany were among the most significant of these.

Hume wrote an essay on suicide around 1755. He intended to publish it, together with another essay, under the title *Essays on Suicide and the Immortality of the Soul*. At the last minute he changed his mind and ordered the work destroyed, either because he felt that the essays did not represent his best thinking or because he expected that his views on suicide would provoke outrage, perhaps even legal trouble. A few copies of the work survived, however, and the essays were published in France in 1770. They did not appear in Great Britain until 1777, a year after Hume's death, and his name was not publicly attached to them until 1783.

Outrage was indeed one reaction to Hume's essay on suicide. Bishops and literary magazines alike condemned it. Other readers and writers, though, agreed with Hume's views, or at least found them worth considering. Hume argued that suicide does not defy the natural order or offend God. It was absurd, he said, to think that any human action could "disturb the order of the world, or invade the business of Providence [God's plan]!" As for the argument that suicide harms society, Hume questioned whether someone whose life has become a burden through illness or misfortune is really useful to society. Perhaps the true benefit to society, he suggested, would come when such people chose to remove themselves from it through suicide. On the overall issue of making moral decisions about suicide, Hume's essay was a step toward replacing institutional authority, such as the dictates of religion or social pressure, with individual autonomy and responsibility.

Voltaire addressed the subject of suicide in a number of works. He was interested in people who killed themselves, and he tried to catalog the reasons for suicide so that he could understand the phenomenon. Although he felt nothing but scorn for the absurd laws that inflicted punishment on the corpses and families of self-murderers, Voltaire sometimes took a lighthearted or witty tone when discussing suicide. For example, he wrote that suicide was only for unsociable people, and that amiable, or likable, people should never kill themselves. He also cautioned the young against killing themselves, because they do not realize how quickly people's circumstances and spirits can change.

In general, however, Voltaire regarded suicide as a matter of individual liberty. No one had the right to question the choice of anyone who was driven to such a measure. Historian of suicide Georges Minois sums up Voltaire's attitude this way: "He advised his friends against it, but he sympathized with those who took that route."

The German philosopher Kant took a much less lenient approach to suicide than Hume and Voltaire. Kant's chief interest was moral philosophy. Confronted with the trends of the Enlightenment—a growing emphasis on individual liberty, and the rise of scientific explanations of the natural world—Kant wrestled with the question of how to know what is right. On the question of suicide, Kant argued that suicide is not a moral act because the reasons for it, such as the desire to avoid pain, dishonor, or dependency, are self-interested, or selfish. To Kant, self-interest could not be the basis for a right or moral act, because the true basis of morality was duty, and suicide violated the duty to preserve oneself in both good and bad times. Kant warned that even suicides that appear noble or self-sacrificing may, if closely examined, prove to have had self-interested motives.

The Good Death

Suicide was universally condemned throughout the Middle Ages. New views of suicide appeared during the Enlightenment, but the great majority of people still believed that it was wrong. Yet historians who have combed through hundreds of years' worth of letters, journals, published literature, and city and town records have learned that all during those centuries, people committed suicide. Ordinary people as well as physicians undoubtedly committed euthanasia, too, by hastening the deaths of those who were dying in pain, although early records of this are very rare. Those who performed such acts would not have called them euthanasia, because that term had a different meaning before the twentieth century.

Euthanasia comes from the Greek words for "the good death." People used it to describe the kind of death everyone hoped to have: peaceful, painless, with one's spiritual and financial affairs in order. Ideally such a death would take place at home, with loved ones and friends, and possibly the family clergyman, doctor, and lawyer, gathered around the bedside. Some people did die this way. Some still do, even in twenty-first-century America, where the majority of deaths take place in hospitals or other care facilities. By the nineteenth century many physicians considered it part of their duty to their patients to help them achieve this good death.

In an 1887 medical textbook titled *Euthanasia*, a British physician named William Munk described the proper role of a doctor when a patient is dying: "We dismiss all thought of cure, or of the prolongation of life, and our efforts are limited to the relief of certain urgent conditions, such as pain." In other words, the physician should not interfere with the course of a "natural" death, either by making a doomed effort to keep the patient alive or by actively ending the patient's life. At the same time physicians administered narcotics and painkillers such as morphine and alcohol to their patients with a generous hand in order to relieve pain. When patients were clearly terminal or dying, doctors did not worry about fostering drug addiction—a concern that makes many modern physicians limit pain medication, even for terminally ill patients. If the physician's duty was to strike a balance between prolonging life and hastening death, some physicians knowingly tipped that balance. They gave their dying patients doses of medication that they knew would be lethal. Today this is known as the "double effect." In earlier times it was something that doctors did occasionally, usually at a patient's request, but did not discuss openly. Such physicians did provide aid in dying, and not just for terminally ill or gravely injured patients. Infants born with severe deformities might be given a strong dose of medication to ease them quietly out of life, especially if doctors considered them unlikely to survive.

Even before Dr. Munk published his book, euthanasia had begun to take on its modern meaning, shifting from "the good death" to "ending life to end suffering." In 1870 an English schoolteacher named Samuel D. Williams launched a debate about active euthanasia, or "mercy killing," with a magazine article that was widely reprinted and discussed. Williams argued in favor of euthanasia, saying that a society that was willing to execute criminals and send soldiers into deadly combat had no right to take a moral stand against providing a painless death for dying patients who were in terrible pain—patients who begged for an end to their suffering. In such circumstances, Williams claimed, euthanasia would be compassionate.

As more people spoke and wrote about euthanasia, physicians and medical organizations joined the debate. For most medical practitioners the key issue was the difference between passive and active euthanasia—between letting someone die, sometimes expressed as "letting nature take its course," and actively hastening death. According to the highly respected *Boston Medical and Surgical Journal* (later called the *New England Journal of Medicine*), it was perfectly proper for a doctor to let a patient die by refusing to use extreme measures to prolong the patient's life. Deliberately shortening a patient's life, however, was wrong in principle and should not be legalized, even though it was an open secret in medical circles that it sometimes happened.

As early as 1906 a legislator in Ohio made the first effort to legalize euthanasia in the United States. He presented a bill to the state legislature that described what today would be called physician-assisted suicide. If the bill became law, a physician could offer a painless death to any patient who was terminally ill or suffering extreme pain without prospect of relief. The patient would have to testify before witnesses that he or she wanted to die, and three physicians would have to agree that the patient's medical condition met the qualifications of the law. The bill never even came to a vote, but it placed the issue of active euthanasia in the realm of public and political debate.

A similar attempt was made to legalize euthanasia in the British city of Leicester in the 1930s. It failed, but it spurred the organization of the British Voluntary Euthanasia Society, founded in 1935. The society's membership included a number of famous intellectuals, including novelist H. G. Wells, playwright George Bernard Shaw, and philosopher and mathematician Bertrand Russell. Three years later the Euthanasia Society of America (ESA) was formed in New York. The ESA tried, and failed, to pass a euthanasia law in New York.

Despite the failure of early attempts to legalize euthanasia, public opinion polls in the 1930s showed that significant portions of the population in both the United States and Great Britain supported some form of voluntary euthanasia for the incurably or terminally ill. One Gallup poll in the United States, for example, found that 46 per-

m. H. G. Wells, prophet and idealist,

THIS CARICATURE OF H. G. WELLS SHOWS HIM USHERING IN HIS
VERSION OF FUTURE BABIES. THE CAPTION READS, "H. G. WELLS,
PROPHET AND IDEALIST, CONJURING UP THE DARLING FUTURE." THE
IDEALS THAT LED TO THE ORGANIZATION OF EUTHANASIA SOCIETIES IN
THE WESTERN WORLD DID NOT SURVIVE WORLD WAR II BECAUSE
OF THE HORRORS PERPETRATED BY THE NAZIS.

cent of Americans were in favor of "mercy deaths under Government supervision for hopeless invalids." Events in Germany, however, soon called attention to the dark side of euthanasia.

Modern Nightmares

Starting in 1939 the Nazi government of Germany carried out a program of crimes against humanity under the banner of euthanasia. With the cooperation of many doctors, the Nazis executed mentally handicapped children, then adults with mental or physical handicaps—people whom Germany's leaders considered to have *lebensunwerten lebens*, or "life unworthy of life." This program, in which an estimated 100,000 Germans died, paved the way for the Nazis to declare other groups "unworthy of life." The Nazis went on to execute millions of Jews, homosexuals, and other minorities in the large-scale, highly organized system of killing that is known as the Holocaust.

The Nazi atrocities were based in part on theories of eugenics. The idea behind eugenics is that "good breeding" improves or purifies a population, while "bad breeding" degrades it. Believers in eugenics argued that "sound" human specimens—examples of good mental and physical health, or people who met some racial or genetic standard—should be encouraged to reproduce. "Unsound" specimens should be discouraged from reproducing. The Nazis chose a very thorough form of discouragement: extermination.

Eugenics was not new; people had been discussing various aspects of the idea since the nineteenth century. Nor were the Nazis the first to put it into practice. The fairly common practice of letting severely deformed newborns die was a form of eugenics in action, although it was often motivated by compassion for the infants or their parents.

The Bollinger case in Chicago in 1915 showed that the idea of euthanasia for the disabled had significant support in the United States. A baby named Allan Bollinger had been born with multiple deformities and needed surgery to live. A surgeon named Harry Haiselden advised the parents not to have the surgery performed. They followed Haiselden's advice and the baby died several days later. Haiselden wrote, lectured, and appeared in a movie about the case, hoping to generate support for legalizing euthanasia. He told a reporter that his choice not to operate on the Bollinger baby was based on eugenics, yet there was another reason as well. Haiselden was appalled by the horrifying conditions he had seen in institutions such as homes for the mentally retarded. Letting severely impaired babies die, he believed, was better than dooming them to institutional life.

A number of well-known Americans spoke out in support of Haiselden. Among those who shared his views were attorney Clarence Darrow, novelist Jack London, socialist political leader Eugene V. Debs, the editors of the *New Republic* magazine, and Helen Keller, herself blind, deaf, and dumb, who said, "Our puny sentimentalism has caused us to forget that a human life is sacred only when it may be of some use to itself and to the world." (In the 1980s a similar case in Indiana, known as the Baby Doe case after a mentally retarded newborn who was allowed to starve to death in the hospital, would lead the federal government to pass laws that defined the refusal of life support to a deformed or disabled newborn as child abuse, and therefore illegal, in most cases.)

Whatever support the idea of euthanasia might have had in the early years of the twentieth century was drastically eroded by World War II (1939–1945), after which the Nazi Holocaust was brought to light. By fusing eugenics and murderous forced euthanasia, the Nazis' nightmarish belief system created a terrible public-relations problem for supporters of voluntary euthanasia in the United States and elsewhere. After the facts of the Holocaust became known to the outside world, the ESA and similar groups tried to explain that they favored euthanasia only when it was in the interest of the patient.

Yet some euthanasia supporters still believed in eugenics. Dr. Foster Kennedy, president of the ESA, declared in a speech to the American Psychiatric Association in 1941 that although he opposed euthanasia for any sick person who might "get well and help the world for years after," he favored euthanasia for "Nature's mistakes"—people such as the mentally defective, who should never have been born and who should be freed of their burdensome lives. Such statements did nothing to advance the cause of euthanasia.

With the word *euthanasia* tainted by association with the Nazis and eugenics, people looked for new terminology. In a 1949 case that received national publicity, a physician named Hermann Sander was charged with murder after he hastened the death of a comatose, dying cancer patient. Sander's act was generally referred to as a "mercy killing" by those who approved of what he had done as well as those who disapproved.

In the end Sander was acquitted. Soon afterward an article in the *New Republic* magazine pointed out, "If we called these situations 'assisted suicide' rather than 'mercy killing,' the moral context would be considerably changed." A few years later, as part of a 1956 article on euthanasia, *Time* magazine quoted a San Francisco physician as saying, "There has been too little said of a legitimate right, a God-given right, of the dying man. That is his right to die." A new vocabulary for debates about the end of life was taking shape.

During the second half of the twentieth century, as the

horrors of the Nazi Holocaust began to recede into the past, the industrialized world faced a new kind of nightmare. This time the culprit was modern medicine, one of the centerpieces of scientific achievement and Western civilization. Medical research and technology had accomplished remarkable things. Antibiotics and other newly developed drugs had brought seemingly miraculous cures for infectious illnesses that once ravaged whole populations. Advances in lifesaving equipment and procedures had snatched many people back from the brink of death. Yet progress had its perils. The invention of respirators and feeding tubes that could keep a body alive long past the point of natural death, even when the mind had ceased to function, gave rise to the fear of being helplessly trapped in a prolonged existence somewhere between life and death. That fear, and several widely publicized cases of people in such situations, helped shape the current debate over the right to die.

3
The Right to Die Goes Public

In 1957 a woman wrote an anonymous article for *Atlantic Monthly* magazine, describing her husband's death in an urban hospital. She called it "a new way of dying . . . the slow passage via modern medicine." She also called it "torture": multiple surgeries, machines to breathe for him, tubes to put food into his stomach, repeated lapses into unconsciousness followed by medications that woke him up, all in a useless attempt to defeat death, or at least to fight it for as long as possible.

A surgeon named Dr. John Farrell read and reflected on the article. The following year, in a speech to a meeting of the American College of Surgeons, Farrell called upon medical professionals to examine the way new technology was changing the experience of dying for patients and their families. He said:

In our pursuit of the scientific aspects of science, the art of medicine has sometimes unwittingly and unjustifiably suffered. . . . The deathbed scenes I

witness are not particularly dignified. The family is shoved out into the corridor by the physical presence of intravenous stands, suction machines, oxygen tanks and tubes emanating from every natural and several surgically induced orifices. The last words . . . are lost behind an oxygen mask.

Farrell was not the only physician who expressed unease over the keep-the-patient-alive-at-any-cost direction of medicine. Articles and letters published in medical journals, newspapers, and magazines echoed the same theme.

Religious leaders and thinkers also entered the conversation about death in the modern world. The Roman Catholic Church, a steadfast opponent of suicide and euthanasia, had traditionally championed life over death in all situations. In 1957 an organization of medical professionals called the International Congress of Anesthesiology asked the pope for guidance in the matter of resuscitating patients—that is, attempting to bring them back to life or consciousness. Acknowledging that modern medicine had created new conditions of dying, Pope Pius XII replied that families and medical caregivers should take all ordinary steps to preserve life, but were not required to use "extraordinary" measures, such as respirators, to prolong it. The pope also told physicians that it was the family's right to authorize the use or withdrawal of such extraordinary measures.

In effect the church had authorized passive euthanasia, or letting someone die, in some circumstances. Assisted suicide and active euthanasia remained forbidden, but the church continued to permit the "double effect"—the use of medication such as narcotics to relieve pain, even though the physician knew that the medication would also lead to death. In 1980 Pope John Paul II went one step further. Declaring that the church no longer saw a difference

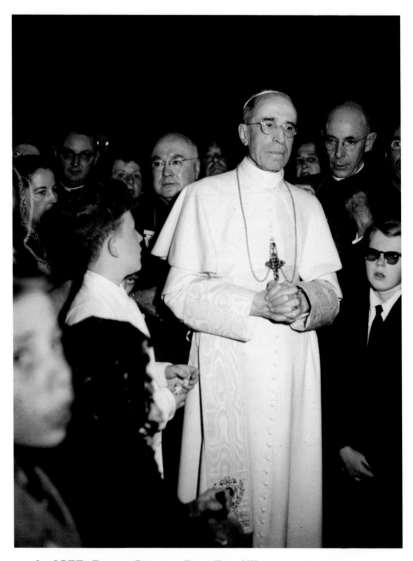

IN 1957, ROMAN CATHOLIC POPE PIUS XII TOOK THE POSITION THAT IT WAS ACCEPTABLE FOR A DYING PATIENT TO REFUSE "EXTRAORDINARY" MEASURES; MORE RECENTLY, THE AMERICAN CATHOLIC CHURCH HAS TAKEN THE SIDE OF THOSE WHO BELIEVE THAT EXTRAORDINARY MEASURES SHOULD INDEED BE TAKEN TO PROLONG LIFE.

between ordinary and extraordinary medical treatment to prolong life, he said that it was acceptable for a dying patient to refuse any medical treatment.

Trends in Dying

The 1960s and 1970s brought a surge of interest in death. Once discussed in whispers or avoided as a taboo subject, death was now the subject of a string of books. Some of these books were memoirs by dying people or their families. One of the first to be widely read was *Death of a Man* (1957), in which Lael Wertenbaker chronicled her husband's decision to end his life on his own terms during the final stage of terminal liver cancer. Wertenbaker reported a confrontation she had with their physician after her husband chose not to have an operation that would have provided only temporary relief:

> **"You cannot let him refuse!" [Dr. Cartier] said. "You're responsible. You're the well one. You and I should take him by force if necessary in an ambulance to the hospital. You cannot leave it to him. . . ."**

> **"If he wants it, we'll do it," I said, raising my voice as Cartier had raised his, tried almost beyond my own endurance. "It's his body, his life, his mind! His pain. He's not nuts or weak-minded. He is a man. He can do as he pleases."**

When Charles Wertenbaker's pain became unbearable, he committed suicide at home by injecting himself with morphine and cutting his wrists.

The Wertenbakers' decision reflected a general demand on the part of patients to have a greater say in their medical treatment, including end-of-life treatment. People were becoming less willing to regard physicians as all-knowing figures who should make decisions for them. Instead of having their doctors tell them what to do, more and more people were insisting on being fully informed about their conditions and choices, and on making decisions for themselves. In response the American Medical Association (AMA) published a Patient's Bill of Rights in 1973. Among those rights was the right to refuse treatment.

Coupled with this trend was a growing interest in the social, cultural, and psychological meanings of death. *On Death and Dying* (1969), by a psychiatrist named Elisabeth Kübler-Ross, became a best seller. In addition to paving the way for other books about death and grief, the book led many readers to explore their own ideas, beliefs, and fears about dying.

Another trend in dying began in London in 1967, when a physician named Cicely Saunders revived an old idea and founded Saint Christopher's, the first hospice in the modern world. Hospices had existed during the Middle Ages. Typically run by members of religious orders, they were places of rest for people on religious pilgrimages and also for the dying. Saunders wanted Saint Christopher's to be a place where terminally ill people could die in comfort. Treatment was aimed not at battling illness or prolonging life but at palliative or comfort care, which meant easing a dying person's pain and anxiety through whatever was helpful: pain medication, psychological and family counseling, religious services, and more. Saunders described the purpose of hospice as "easing the pain of dying or allowing someone to die when the time comes."

The first hospice in the United States was established in Connecticut in 1974. The following year a medical and legal case grabbed headlines across the country and around the world. It would influence the growth of the

ELISABETH KÜBLER-ROSS BECAME FAMOUS AS THE AUTHOR OF THE FIVE STAGES OF GRIEF—DENIAL, ANGER, BARGAINING, DEPRESSION, AND ACCEPTANCE—OUTLINED IN HER BOOK, *ON DEATH AND DYING*. SINCE THEN, THE FIVE STAGES HAVE BEEN INCORPORATED INTO COMEDY ROUTINES, AND EVEN INTO AN EPISODE OF *THE SOPRANOS*.

hospice movement in America as well as other attitudes, practices, and laws related to death.

The Quinlan Case

In April 1975 a twenty-one-year-old New Jersey woman named Karen Ann Quinlan lost consciousness after drinking and taking drugs at a party. Quinlan fell into a coma and was hospitalized, with a breathing tube from a respirator down her throat and feeding tubes into her stomach. After six weeks Robert Morse, a specialist in brain and nervous system disorders who had been treating Quinlan, told her parents that she was in a persistent vegetative state (PVS), meaning that she had suffered serious brain damage and would not regain consciousness. After consulting with their Roman Catholic priest, who explained the pope's 1957 ruling on "extraordinary means" of prolonging life, the Quinlans decided that the shriveled, unconscious body in their daughter's hospital bed was dead in every way that mattered. They formally requested Morse to disconnect Karen's respirator. Morse and the Catholic hospital refused, claiming that to do so would amount to euthanasia, an immoral and illegal act.

A central issue in the Quinlan case was the question of proxy, or acting on behalf of someone else. Karen Ann Quinlan was not refusing life support—her parents were refusing it for her. Yet Karen was an adult, which meant that her parents lacked the legal authority to make decisions on her behalf. The Quinlans asked a New Jersey judge to name Joe Quinlan as his daughter's guardian and to grant specific permission for Quinlan to have the respirator disconnected.

Julia Quinlan testified that her daughter had told her on more than one occasion that she would not want to be kept alive artificially. The Quinlans' attorney argued that the family's decision outweighed that of the doctor and hospital. He cited laws and earlier court decisions that guaranteed a right to privacy in matters of medical care and control over one's body, such as the 1973 decision by the U.S. Supreme Court in *Roe* v. *Wade* that made abortion legal. On the other side Morse and Karen's temporary court-appointed guardian argued that their duty to the patient, who had not made her own views clear before the coma claimed her, was to keep her alive.

The judge agreed with Morse. He denied Joe Quinlan's request to be made his daughter's guardian, and he declared that she must remain connected to the respirator. Although he acknowledged that Karen Ann Quinlan could have refused treatment for herself, he ruled that a parent could not claim a constitutional right to die on behalf of an adult child, even if that child was now incapable of making a decision.

The Quinlans appealed the judge's ruling to the New Jersey Supreme Court. In March 1976 the court overturned the judge's earlier decision, declaring that the right to privacy did apply to the Quinlan case. The court named Joe Quinlan as Karen's guardian. Still the hospital refused to remove the respirator at Quinlan's request, which was *its* right. While the Quinlans made arrangements to move Karen to a different care facility where Joe Quinlan's request would be followed, the staff at the hospital began turning off Karen's respirator for short periods to see whether Karen's body could get used to breathing on its own. By the time Karen's parents relocated her and disconnected the respirator, she was able to breathe. She never regained consciousness, but the Quinlans decided not to remove the tubes that administered food and antibiotics. To do so, they felt, would cross the line from letting Karen die to euthanizing her—a step they were unwilling to take.

Karen Ann Quinlan lingered in her coma in a nursing home until 1986, when she died of pneumonia. In the meantime her parents found a way to honor her. After a visit to Saint Christopher's, the pioneer hospice in London, the Quinlans founded a nonprofit hospice organization to send caregivers into the homes of the terminally ill in northern New Jersey.

When the Karen Ann Quinlan Center of Hope was founded in 1980, it was one of sixty hospice services in the United States. That number increased dramatically in a very short period of time—there were eight hundred programs by 1982. Since then the number of hospice providers has continued to grow. Several nonprofit organizations now operate nationwide networks of nurses, counselors, and other caregivers who provide palliative care in patients' homes, hospitals, nursing homes, or facilities dedicated to hospice use. Medicare, a federally administered health-insurance program, covers the cost of hospice for patients with fewer than six months to live.

The hospice movement, designed to ease the transition from life to death for both dying people and their families, continues to gain recognition from physicians as having a role to play in the overall world of medicine. Care that focuses on the patient's comfort rather than on battling the disease is now a possibility for many people who are terminally ill. It is also an alternative to suicide or voluntary euthanasia, for these options are not part of the hospice philosophy. Opponents of assisted suicide hope that further growth of the hospice movement, along with programs to educate physicians and patients about it, will mean that people will be less afraid of pain and the process of dying. If so, they may be more willing to live out their days to the end rather than feeling driven to meet death ahead of schedule.

The Rise of Advance Directives

In the storm of publicity and controversy that surrounded the Karen Ann Quinlan case from 1975 to 1976, many Americans heard for the first time about advance health-care directives. An advance health-care directive is a document in which a mentally competent adult gives instructions about his or her future health care under certain circumstances. If someone who has prepared a directive later becomes incompetent to make health-care decisions, the directive tells what decisions he or she would have made.

The living will was the first type of advance health-care directive that was introduced in the United States. A living will is a document in which a competent adult can specify what medical treatments should be given or withheld if that person later becomes unable to make or communicate decisions. The living will may also detail circumstances in which the person would want all medical treatment to cease. A living will can indicate, for example, whether someone would ever want to be attached to a respirator or feeding tube, or to a dialysis machine to replace failed kidneys, and for how long.

Living wills were first suggested in 1969, but few people prepared them. There were no laws to enforce living wills, which meant that family members, doctors, and hospitals were not required to follow them if they did not want to. Laws to make living wills legally binding had been introduced in several state legislatures in 1974, but none had passed. Two years later, after the Quinlan case, California became the first state to pass a law that gave living wills the force of legally binding documents. Other states followed.

Another type of advance health-care directive, the durable power of attorney for health care, soon appeared. This directive is sometimes called a health-care proxy because it names a proxy, someone who will have the legal authority to make health-care decisions on behalf of the person who prepared the directive. The proxy may be a spouse or relative, but does not have to be.

Health-care proxies are broader in scope and stronger in force than living wills. Living wills concern what are sometimes called deathbed decisions: questions about artificial life support for the terminally ill or dying. A durable power of attorney for health care, or health-care proxy, goes into effect whenever the person who prepared the directive is unable to make any health-care decision, such as during surgery or temporary unconsciousness. A durable power of attorney for health care overrides a living will if the terms of the two documents are in conflict. It is harder for someone who disagrees with a patient's wishes to ignore a health-care proxy than to ignore a living will because the proxy appoints an agent who must actively enforce the patient's wishes. The agent has the power to accept or refuse treatment, choose health-care facilities and physicians, and authorize or refuse organ donation on behalf of the patient.

A third type of advance directive is the "Do Not Resuscitate" order, or DNR. These directives, which were made legally binding in the 1980s, came into wider use in the 1990s. The DNR is used in a health-care setting, such as a hospital or nursing home. A patient or proxy can request that a DNR order be placed on the patient's chart. This means that if the patient's heart stops beating, the staff cannot attempt to restart it using cardiopulmonary resuscitation (CPR) techniques. Although studies have found that doctors or patients' families sometimes ignore or override DNRs (and living wills as well), such incidents are becoming less common as patients become better informed about their rights—and as hospitals face lawsuits from patients whose legally binding orders were not followed.

In 1990 the U.S. Congress passed a federal law called the Patient Self-Determination Act (PSDA). It requires care institutions such as hospitals, nursing homes, and health management organizations (HMOs) to provide patients with written copies of their health-care rights, including the right to have an advance health-care directive. Institutions are also required to ask new patients whether they have health-care directives, but they are not allowed to treat patients differently depending on whether or not the patients have directives. Although the PSDA is a federal law, each state has its own laws regarding advance health-care directives. Some states require living wills or health-care proxies to be witnessed or notarized, for example, and in some states living wills are void for women who are pregnant.

The Right-to-Die Movement

As interest in patients' rights and advance health-care directives increased, another movement was taking shape, one that was dedicated to helping the terminally ill do more than say when the respirator should be disconnected. The right-to-die movement was made up of individuals and organizations that spoke out in favor of people's freedom to control their own deaths and end their lives through suicide, assisted suicide, or active euthanasia.

Suicide, once a crime throughout the Western world, had been decriminalized in most places. France repealed its antisuicide laws in 1789, during the French Revolution. The United Kingdom did not do so until 1961, making it one of the last nations in which suicide and attempted suicide carried legal penalties. In the United States, various states had passed laws making suicide or attempted suicide a felony, but these laws were almost never enforced. Most of them were repealed during the nineteenth century, although a few of them lingered on the books until late in the twentieth century.

The decriminalization of suicide reflected a new view of the act, one that placed it within a medical context. Suicide had come to be seen as a sign of insanity, depression, or another type of mental disturbance. As a result, although suicide was not an illegal act, someone who tried to commit suicide but failed might be required to undergo medical or psychiatric treatment, possibly even involuntary confinement in a mental hospital. It was widely accepted as

fact—an obvious fact, to most people's way of thinking—
that anyone who considered ending his or her life must be
mentally disturbed. The right-to-die movement wanted to
change that. It argued that under certain circumstances,
such as unending pain or terminal decay, the decision to
end life could be not only permissible but reasonable.

In 1978, two years after the final court ruling in the
Quinlan case, a British man named Derek Humphry published a book titled *Jean's Way*. It described his first wife's
decision to take her own life, with Humphry's assistance,
rather than die a lingering, painful death from cancer.
British authorities could have prosecuted Humphry under
a law against assisting a suicide, but they decided not to.
Humphry moved to the United States where, with his second wife, he founded the Hemlock Society in 1980. Many
historians of the modern right-to-die movement in America consider the creation of the Hemlock Society to be
its beginning.

Named for the poison that Socrates drank in ancient
Athens, the Hemlock Society set itself apart from older organizations such as the Euthanasia Society of America.
The earlier groups had focused on philosophical discussions of individual rights and on political activism, such as
trying to get euthanasia legalized. The Hemlock Society
shared the goal of legalizing assisted suicide and active voluntary euthanasia for the terminally ill, but it went further.
It wanted to educate people about the practical aspects of
what Humphry called "self-deliverance"—in other words,
tell people how to kill themselves efficiently and painlessly.

Humphry and other members of the Hemlock Society
defined two kinds of suicide: emotional and rational. Emotional suicide is "irrational self-murder in all its complexi-
ties," as Humphry described it—suicide for emotional
or mental-health reasons. Such suicides should be pre-
vented whenever possible, never encouraged. Rational

suicide, in contrast, was "justifiable suicide"—planned self-deliverance, or self-euthanasia, for good reasons. In the Hemlock Society's view, those good reasons were "advanced terminal illness that is causing unbearable suffering to the individual" and "grave physical handicap so restricting that the individual cannot, even after due consideration and training, tolerate such a limited existence." The Hemlock Society was formed to help people in those situations who had decided upon rational suicide.

The first step in this direction was Humphry's 1981 book *Let Me Die Before I Wake*, a collection of factual

THE HEMLOCK SOCIETY CHAMPIONS THE RIGHT OF THE TERMINALLY ILL TO CHOOSE WHEN TO END LIFE. IN JANUARY 1997 MEMBERS OF THE SOCIETY DEMONSTRATED IN FRONT OF THE U.S. SUPREME COURT IN FAVOR OF ASSISTED SUICIDE. THE SUPREME COURT JUSTICES DID NOT AGREE.

accounts of people who had killed themselves or a loved one as an alternative to end-of-life suffering. A reader could glean from these accounts information about effective and ineffective methods of death, as well as details such as proper drug dosages. At first only members of the Hemlock Society could obtain the book, but it was later made available to the general public.

Humphry's next book, *Final Exit* (1991), was a straightforward how-to manual for suicides and their assistants. It was Humphry's belief that any terminally ill person who was resolved to die deserved to be spared the frustration—and the possible disastrous outcome—of unsuccessful or botched suicide attempts. He was determined to make the simple facts about various ways of exiting life available to readers.

Final Exit outraged and alarmed people who feared that it would encourage suicide, and not just by the terminally ill. Some of the strongest critics of the book were members of the right-to-life movement, which had formed to oppose legalized abortion but extended its concern to euthanasia as well. Yet *Final Exit* also aroused curiosity, and it offered comfort to people who simply wanted to know that they possessed the power to terminate their lives, even if they never used it. The book was on the *New York Times* best-seller list for more than four months. It has remained in print, occasionally updated, ever since. Derek Humphry has remained a vocal supporter of a terminally ill person's right to die. He now lives in Oregon and heads the Euthanasia Research and Guidance Organization (ERGO).

A Constitutional Question

A legal confrontation brought the issue of the right to die before the U.S. Supreme Court in 1989. Like the Karen

Ann Quinlan case, the case of Nancy Cruzan involved a young woman who was in a persistent vegetative state and was being kept alive by artificial nutrition and hydration (ANH), or food and water administered by tubes. In 1983, when Cruzan was twenty-five, her car slid off the road one winter night in her home state of Missouri. Before emergency rescue teams arrived, Cruzan lay facedown in a ditch filled with water for fifteen minutes. Paramedics managed to restart her heart and breathing, but she had suffered brain damage and did not regain consciousness. Her parents, Joe and Joyce Cruzan, placed her in a state hospital where she was cared for at the state's expense.

After four years the Cruzans were certain that their daughter's condition would never improve. They told the hospital staff to remove her ANH tubes and let her die. The staff refused. The Cruzans took their case to a judge, as the Quinlans had done before them. The judge granted the Cruzans permission to order Nancy's tubes removed, but the Missouri Department of Health, seeking to keep Nancy alive, appealed the case to the state supreme court.

The state supreme court overturned the judge's ruling in a 4 to 3 vote. The court declared that the state had a fundamental interest in preserving the life of its citizens. That interest could give way only to clear and convincing evidence that the patient would have wanted to die. Nancy Cruzan had not prepared an advance health-care directive. The only evidence of her position on medical treatment came from one housemate's memory of a conversation. In the eyes of the court, this evidence was not sufficiently clear or convincing.

The Cruzans then appealed the case to the highest court in the land, the U.S. Supreme Court, which heard arguments from both sides in December 1989. Nearly six months later the Court announced its opinion in the case of *Cruzan v. Director, Missouri Department of Health*. In a majority opinion written by Chief Justice William H. Rehnquist, the Court said, "This is the first case in which we have been squarely presented with the issue of whether the United States Constitution grants what is in common parlance referred to as a 'right to die.'"

The Supreme Court assumed for the purposes of the *Cruzan* case, based on laws and earlier court decisions, that "the United States Constitution would grant a competent person a constitutionally protected right to refuse lifesaving nutrition and hydration." This right must also extend to people who were incompetent, as long as they had made their wishes known while they were competent. This was the first time the Supreme Court had acknowledged a constitutional right to die, even in limited terms (the Court did not discuss any form of voluntary death beyond the refusal of treatment such as ANH).

The Court's attention then turned to the question of whether the state of Missouri had a constitutional right to require evidence of a patient's wishes and to set the standards for that evidence. The justices held that the state did have such a right. Missouri was allowed to decide that the evidence the Cruzans had presented of their daughter's wishes was not strong enough to warrant ending ANH. The ruling of the state supreme court was upheld. Nancy would remain on life support.

The Cruzan story did not end there. The publicity surrounding the case had caught the attention of several people who had known Nancy. They testified in a Missouri court hearing that they had had conversations with her in which she had said she would not wish to be kept alive by feeding and hydration tubes. Representatives of the state accepted this as clear and convincing evidence, and the judge's original ruling—that Nancy's tubes could be removed—was allowed to stand. Nancy Cruzan's ANH was withdrawn in December 1990. More than a dozen members of a right-to-life group called Operation Rescue came to the hospital on a mission to reinsert Cruzan's feeding tubes; the confrontation ended in their arrest. Cruzan died after eleven days, never having shown any sign of consciousness.

While the Cruzans waited to hear the Supreme Court's ruling on their daughter's case, tragedy struck another young woman. Her name was Terri Schiavo, and in time she would become the center of a storm of controversy. In February 1990 the twenty-six-year-old Schiavo suffered cardiac arrest (stopping of the heartbeat) in her home in Florida. Medical intervention restarted Schiavo's breathing and heartbeat, but the time without oxygen had caused brain damage. Schiavo was in a coma for longer than two months. After that she returned to a cycle of waking and sleeping, but she showed no inarguable signs that she was aware of herself or anything around her. She had to be fed through a tube; eventually it was surgically inserted into her stomach.

Schiavo was cared for in nursing homes. For the first few years she received therapy aimed at treating or rehabilitating her—in other words, helping her regain some degree of consciousness and memory. A series of physicians diagnosed her as being in a persistent vegetative state, with little or no hope of any recovery. In 1998 Schiavo's husband asked a judge to rule on whether Terri's feeding and hydration tubes could be removed, letting her die. The judge ruled that they could, sparking a seven-year battle. On one side were Michael Schiavo and those who supported his right to end Terri's life; on the other were her parents, who believed that she showed consciousness at times and could be rehabilitated, and those who supported their desire to keep Terri alive. People and groups from both the right-to-die and right-to-life camps issued hundreds of statements and opinions while the Schiavo case wound its way through a series of legal battles. The case never reached the U.S. Supreme Court. The Court turned down four requests to hear the case because the justices felt that there were no valid grounds for it to get involved. All of the issues raised in the case were covered under the existing body of law and previous judicial decisions.

The central question in the Schiavo conflict, as in the Quinlan and Cruzan cases, was: Who had the right to make health-care decisions for someone who could no longer make them for herself but had left no written guidelines? In the Schiavo case Terri's parents argued that she would have wanted to stay alive, while her husband claimed that she would not have wanted a prolonged existence on life support in a vegetative state. The case was complicated by disputes about the nature of Schiavo's condition.

In 2003, after a court order allowed Terri's feeding tube to be removed, the Schiavo case shifted from a legal to a political issue. The Florida legislature hastily passed a law, signed by Governor Jeb Bush, brother of President George W. Bush, that gave the governor authority to order the feeding tube to be reinserted. A circuit court and the Florida state supreme court struck down the law as unconstitutional.

Religion was another element in the Schiavo case. Schiavo came from a Roman Catholic family, and her parents claimed that she would wish to follow Catholic teaching and rules about the end of life. In 2004, undoubtedly in reaction to the Schiavo case, Pope John Paul II declared that under Catholic doctrine, health-care providers cannot deny food and water to patients in vegetative states who cannot make their wishes directly known. Terri's parents tried but failed to obtain a new trial because of this development.

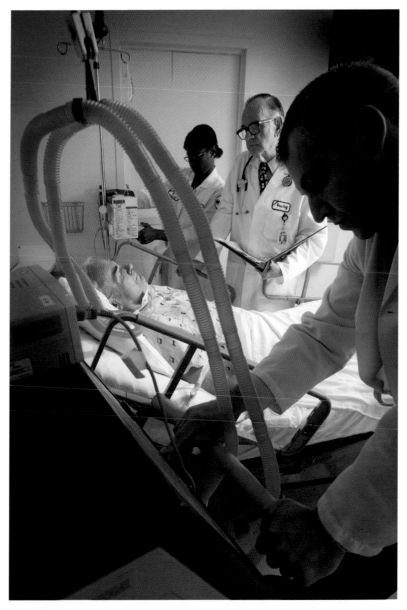

MEDICAL STAFF MONITOR A PATIENT ON A MECHANICAL VENTILATOR.
TODAY, TECHNOLOGY CAN TAKE OVER FOR PATIENTS UNABLE TO
BREATHE ON THEIR OWN.

Doctor Death: Mercitron or Murder Machine?

No figure in the right-to-die movement has been more controversial than a Michigan physician named Jack Kevorkian—or Doctor Death, as some of his critics have called him. His opponents consider Kevorkian a murderer because he did more than talk about assisted suicide. He helped people die.

Kevorkian's involvement in assisted suicide and euthanasia began in the 1980s, when he wrote articles explaining why he believed that physician-assisted suicide and voluntary euthanasia should be legalized. He designed a device he called the Thanatron, or death machine, that would deliver a painless, lethal drug injection at the push of a button. Kevorkian would connect the person seeking death to the Thanatron and provide the drug, but the person would have to press the button on his or her own.

In 1990 Janet Adkins, a woman whose doctors had told her that she was in the early stages of Alzheimer's disease, became the first user of the Thanatron. She had heard about Kevorkian on television and came to Michigan to use his device. Throughout the 1990s Kevorkian continued his crusade to provide a painless death to those who sought it. He designed a second device that he called a Mercitron (mercy machine) that used a gas mask to deliver carbon monoxide, which produces unconsciousness followed by death.

By his own account Kevorkian helped more than a hundred people to die. All of them sought him out, and in each case he obtained written or videotaped records of their consent. His subjects had clearly decided to end their lives before contacting him, and they took the final step in activating his machines. Many of Kevorkian's subjects and their family members offered glowing tributes, thanking him for his courageous help in freeing them from their unbearable lives. Yet Kevorkian's critics—even some who support the right to die—pointed out that he did not talk with his subjects about other ways they might have sought help, such as psychological therapy or hospice care. Nor did he call upon other physicians to confirm the diagnoses of his subjects, whom he did not know well. Many of the subjects were not terminally ill. Several were later found to have no physical disease; they may have suffered from depression.

Kevorkian made no effort to charm the public. His manner, in fact, struck many as arrogant and abrasive. He openly challenged Michigan prosecutors to find him guilty of a crime. The state withdrew Kevorkian's license to practice medicine and made several attempts to convict him of assisted suicide. These attempts ended in "not guilty" verdicts or mistrials. In 1998, in the hope of stopping Kevorkian, Michigan's legislators passed a law that absolutely banned any form of assisted suicide. Kevorkian's last trial, however, would not be for assisted suicide. In 1998 he was charged with second-degree murder in the death of Thomas Youk.

Youk suffered from amyotrophic lateral sclerosis (ALS), a disease that drastically limited his ability to use his hands. He asked for Kevorkian's help in dying but could not activate a machine himself. For the first time Kevorkian agreed to perform the fatal act. He videotaped himself obtaining permission from Youk and then injecting Youk with a drug combination that killed him. Then, with what might be called either arrogant foolishness or a brave wish to educate and arouse the public, Kevorkian arranged for the videotape to be broadcast on the CBS news program *60 Minutes*. Michigan prosecutors promptly charged Kevorkian with murder. The court did not permit Youk's video-taped testimony or that of his family to be admitted as evidence for the defense.

Kevorkian was found guilty and sentenced to ten to twenty-five years in prison. In 2007, after serving eight years and suffering from health problems, he was released. Kevorkian has declared that he will assist in no more suicides, although he continues to support voluntary euthanasia.

By 2005 a new court order had been issued, once again allowing the cessation of Terri Schiavo's ANH. This time the federal government got involved. Congress passed and President Bush signed a law that transferred the Schiavo case from state to federal courts. The federal courts, however, followed the state courts in turning down Terri's parents' efforts to block the court order.

Terri Schiavo died in 2005 after artificial feeding and hydration were stopped. An autopsy performed on her body confirmed that she had indeed suffered massive, irreversible brain damage and had been in a persistent vegetative state. Her death was enormously controversial, yet the central issue was much the same as in the Quinlan and Cruzan cases. Perhaps the Schiavo case received greater media and congressional attention than the earlier cases because it quickly became a conflict not just between Terri's husband and her parents but between opposing social movements and viewpoints. Spokespeople and organizations on both sides of the issue had become good at using heart-wrenching cases to advance their views.

The Next Battleground

As the right-to-die movement developed, more and more accounts of assisted suicides—or people helping their husbands, wives, children, or parents to die—had appeared in books, magazines, and newspapers. Assisting a suicide, unlike suicide itself, was against the law. In the past the courts had dealt with such cases in a highly inconsistent way, depending upon the state, the year, and the circumstances of the case. Some individuals had been prosecuted and convicted for assisting in a suicide. In Michigan in 1920, for example, a man was sentenced to life in prison for preparing a poisonous drink for his dying wife. He was convicted of murder, even though she had wanted to die.

Often, however, prosecutors and courts had taken a lenient view of people who appeared to have acted out of compassion, even in cases of euthanasia rather than suicide. But as the Quinlan and Cruzan cases made headlines, as best-selling books told people how to help other people die, and as the right-to-life movement strengthened its opposition to the right-to-die movement, the states-passed new laws against assisted suicide, or tightened existing laws. As a result suicide was not illegal, but assisting a suicide was.

Some states and nations passed laws specifically forbidding physicians to help their patients die. During the 1990s physician-assisted suicide would become the new battleground in the struggle over the right to die.

4

Assisted Suicide and the Law

"If you disagree with voluntary euthanasia, then don't use it," wrote Bob Dent in a letter that would be shared with the public after his death, "but please don't deny the right to me." Dent was a sixty-six-year-old Australian man who was suffering from terminal cancer. It was 1996, and Dent was about to become the first person in the world to die through legal physician-assisted suicide.

At the time a few countries already had established guidelines under which physician-assisted suicide was tolerated by the law. One state in the United States had passed a law that formally gave physicians the power to help terminal patients die, although that law had not yet come into force. In addition physicians everywhere were helping patients to die quietly, behind the scenes and off the record, as has always been the case.

Bob Dent's case was different. He took advantage of the first law that had ever been enacted to let patients obtain voluntary euthanasia from doctors. That law and others like it, however, have had a stormy history. From the point of view of those who are fighting for the right to die, only a few battles have been won.

The Netherlands: Breaking New Ground

The first country in which physician aid in dying was openly tolerated was The Netherlands. During the second half of the twentieth century, The Netherlands passed laws that allowed and governed controversial practices such as prostitution and the use of certain drugs. Those who oppose assisted suicide regard it as another step on the Dutch road to moral or ethical ruin. Others applaud the Dutch for taking bold steps to regulate assisted suicide. People were doing it anyway, goes one line of thought, so it is better to have it done openly and under examination than secretly. In addition the Dutch have traditionally placed a high value on both tolerance and privacy. This has led to a liberal willingness to let people do what they want as long as they do not harm others.

In 1973 a Dutch physician named Geertruida Postma was asked by her terminally ill mother for a quick and painless death. After repeated requests Postma injected her mother with a lethal dose of morphine. Authorities prosecuted the case, and Postma was convicted of murder, although she received a very light sentence. Barry Rosenfeld, a professor of psychology and historian of the right-to-die movement, reports that there was "widespread acceptance of euthanasia among the Dutch public and lawmakers."

The issue of euthanasia in The Netherlands reached a critical turning point in 1983, when a doctor performed euthanasia on a ninety-five-year-old, disabled, bedridden woman who had asked for death multiple times, including a written request. Criminal charges were brought against the doctor in a case that went all the way to the Dutch supreme court.

The supreme court upheld the ruling of a lower court that had found the doctor not guilty. According to the supreme court, the doctor's duty to relieve his patient's suffering had overbalanced his duty to keep her alive. As a result of this case, the Dutch supreme court decided in 1984 that cases of assisted suicide or euthanasia with the help of physicians would no longer be prosecuted, as long as the physicians followed guidelines drawn up by the Dutch Royal Medical Society. Six years later the Dutch justice ministry formally agreed to this arrangement.

Euthanasia and assisted suicide were still technically unlawful, but they were tolerated if these guidelines were followed: The patient must freely, repeatedly, and consciously request help in dying; the patient must be terminally ill or experiencing unbearable suffering that cannot be relieved; the physician must review the case with another physician before granting the patient's request; and the physician must report all cases of euthanasia or assisted suicide.

The informal agreement on euthanasia in The Netherlands became law in early 2001, when the Dutch Senate voted 46 to 28 to pass a bill that legalized mercy killing (either assisted suicide or voluntary euthanasia, although the majority of Dutch patients have chosen euthanasia at the physician's hand). Under the law patients' requests for death must be based on intolerable suffering, but the patient does not have to be terminally ill. The following year the neighboring nation of Belgium passed a similar law.

Support for the new law was strong among citizens of The Netherlands. According to Els Borst, the nation's health minister, approximately 90 percent of the Dutch population favored the law. There was, however, ample opposition. On the day of the vote anti-euthanasia protesters filled a large square outside the national parliament. One protester, Piet Huurman, belonged to a group called Cry for Life. "The tide will turn back someday," he predicted. "They will realize they have made a terrible mistake."

For years both critics and supporters of physician-assisted suicide and voluntary euthanasia have watched The Netherlands closely, debating what the Dutch have done wrong or right. One persistent critic of the Dutch policy on euthanasia is Herbert Hendin, an American psychiatrist who specializes in treating suicidal patients. He argues against any form of physician aid in dying on the general ground that many patients who seek death suffer from depression that could be treated by therapy or medication; even the terminally ill, he points out, may respond to such treatment, and patients have been known to change their minds about suicide once their depression is relieved.

Hendin has also identified what he considers serious problems with the Dutch practice. According to a series of surveys of physicians carried out by the Dutch government, doctors fail to report some euthanasias, and they also occasionally perform euthanasia without the patient's clear consent. "Virtually every guideline established by the Dutch to regulate euthanasia has been modified or violated with impunity," Hendin said in 1996. Furthermore, in 1994 the country's supreme court ruled that mental suffering could qualify as a reason for granting a patient's euthanasia request. This meant that people seeking death would no longer have to be physically ill; physicians could help those suffering from severe psychiatric or emotional distress to die, as long as a psychiatrist is consulted.

A 2007 article in the *New England Journal of Medicine*, however, reported that some early fears about the Dutch law have not come true. Euthanasia reporting by physicians has improved sharply, and the rate of euthanasia has not increased since the law was passed. Bregje Onwuteaka-Philipsen, a Dutch medical professor and health official, said, "An important goal of the euthanasia law in The Netherlands is to achieve public control of this practice. The increase in the reporting of euthanasia and physician-assisted suicide to the review committees, from 18 percent in 1990, through 41 percent in 1995 and 54 percent in 2001 to 80 percent in 2005, shows that that goal of the law is met."

In 2005 Dutch physicians performed euthanasia on approximately 2,325 people, accounting for 1.7 percent of all deaths in The Netherlands. Another 0.1 percent died by means of physician-assisted suicide. These percentages had fallen slightly from 2.6 and 0.2 percent four years earlier. Slightly more than 7 percent of all 2005 deaths involved continuous sedation—the "double effect" of painkillers being used to hasten death—rather than active euthanasia or physician-assisted suicide; this was up from 5.6 percent in 2001. Around 0.4 percent of deaths were cases of non-voluntary euthanasia, performed without the patient's consent. These included cases in which doctors had to make emergency decisions about patients who could not communicate, cases in which patients had informally expressed a desire for euthanasia but had become incompetent before completing a formal request, and cases in which patients were unable to communicate but doctors believed they were suffering intolerably.

Even Herbert Hendin, who is deeply disturbed by the issues of non-voluntary euthanasia and euthanasia for psychiatric patients, has admitted that "[t]he Dutch have accomplished something they wanted: giving their citizens the reassurance that they will not have to endure an unnecessarily prolonged, painful ending to their lives." People have tried to accomplish the same thing in other places, with limited success.

Oregon: Death with Dignity

During the 1990s right-to-die activists sought to legalize physician-assisted suicide in the United States, working on a state-by-state basis. They focused on the West Coast states for several reasons. Research showed that support for the right to die was stronger among liberal West Coast populations than in some other parts of the country, and people in those states can propose laws and vote on them directly through a type of citizen-driven legislation called the ballot initiative.

Attempts to pass ballot initiatives in Washington State and California failed, perhaps because they authorized euthanasia as well as assisted suicide and because they lacked strong safeguards against abuse. Voters rejected these proposals as too drastic. In 1994 activists tried again in Oregon, with a more limited and carefully thought out proposal. Ballot Measure 16, also called the Death with Dignity Act, authorized only physician-assisted suicide, and only for the terminally ill. To calm Oregonians' fears that their state would become a destination for death-seeking tourists, the measure limited assisted suicide to legal residents of Oregon. Safeguards included a waiting period and mandatory consultations with multiple physicians; in addition the patient must perform the final act independently. Voters accepted Measure 16, but not overwhelmingly. It passed by a statewide vote of 52 to 48 percent.

Oregon had become the first state to legalize physician-assisted suicide, but the right-to-die fight was not over. Activists for the National Right to Life Committee, claiming that the Oregon Death with Dignity Act (DWDA) was unconstitutional, were supported by a federal district court judge in Oregon's capital. He issued an order that blocked the DWDA from taking effect. The law's backers immediately appealed the judge's order, which meant that the case was tied up in court for several years. In early 1997 a U.S. district appeals court unanimously overturned the judge's ruling. Opponents of the DWDA appealed the district court's decision to the U.S. Supreme Court, which did not agree to hear the case. The ruling of the district court stood, and the DWDA went into effect in October of 1997, nearly three years after voters had passed the ballot initiative.

The opponents of the DWDA had failed in court, but they hoped to make their case to Oregon's voters. They had placed Measure 51, an initiative to repeal the DWDA,

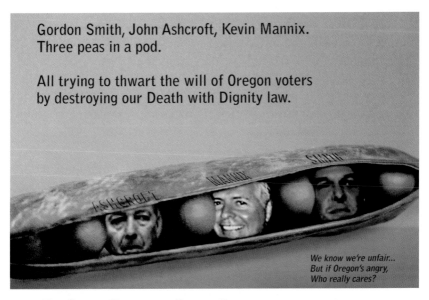

Gordon Smith, John Ashcroft, Kevin Mannix. Three peas in a pod.

All trying to thwart the will of Oregon voters by destroying our Death with Dignity law.

We know we're unfair... But if Oregon's angry, Who really cares?

THE OREGON DEATH WITH DIGNITY ACT IN SOME WAYS MIRRORED KÜBLER-ROSS'S STAGES OF GRIEF, WITH OPPONENTS GOING FROM DENIAL TO, AT BEST, GRUDGING ACCEPTANCE. IN 2002, AFTER THE ACT HAD BEEN STOPPED IN ITS TRACKS, ADVOCATES OF THE LAW SENT A MAILER PORTRAYING ATTORNEY GENERAL JOHN ASHCROFT, SENATE CANDIDATE GORDON SMITH, AND GUBERNATORIAL CANDIDATE KEVIN MANNIX AS THREE PEAS IN A POD.

on the November 1997 ballot, in the hope that Oregonians had changed their minds about assisted suicide. Despite a large advertising campaign funded by several national right-to-life and religious organizations, the voters of Oregon knew what they wanted. Measure 51 failed in a vote of 60 percent to 40 percent. In other words, voters upheld the DWDA by a much wider margin than the original DWDA vote.

The DWDA's troubles continued, however. In 2001 the attorney general of the United States, John Ashcroft, issued a directive ordering a halt to physician-assisted suicide in Oregon. He claimed that the DWDA, which let doctors prescribe lethal doses of pain medication, violated the Controlled Substances Act (CSA), a federal antidrug law. Oregon physicians who assisted suicides, the directive said, faced criminal charges. The state of Oregon responded by suing Ashcroft in a federal district court, which found Ashcroft's directive illegal. The attorney general's office appealed this ruling to a circuit court, which also found the directive illegal. The attorney general's office then appealed to the U.S. Supreme Court, which agreed to hear the case.

The Supreme Court issued its opinion in 2006. By that time Alberto Gonzales had replaced Ashcroft as attorney general. In *Gonzales* v. *Oregon* the Court supported Oregon by a 6-to-3 majority. The justices upheld the ruling of the circuit court that the attorney general's directive was illegal. The CSA did not give the attorney general authority to make rules about physicians' conduct in medical matters that were authorized by state laws.

The DWDA had remained in force in Oregon while the antidrug case was heard, which meant that assisted suicide had been legal for nearly a decade. One requirement of the DWDA is that the Oregon Department of Human Services must maintain and publish annual reports on how the act is being used. The report for 2006 showed that from 1998 through 2006, a total of 292 DWDA deaths had taken place. In every year some of the patients who obtained DWDA prescriptions from their physicians did not use them.

Forty Oregon physicians wrote a total of sixty-five DWDA prescriptions in 2006, and forty-six Oregonians ended their lives using the DWDA. Their deaths accounted for about 0.15 percent of all deaths in Oregon. The people who died under the DWDA in 2006 had a median age of seventy-four. Eighty-seven percent of them suffered from cancer, also the dominant disease in earlier reports. According to patient surveys, their leading concerns about the end of life were the loss of autonomy, the loss of ability to enjoy life, the loss of dignity, and inadequate pain control.

The Supreme Court on Assisted Suicide

When opponents of Oregon's Death with Dignity Act appealed their case to the Supreme Court in 1997, the Court refused to hear the case. The justices did not turn down the Oregon case because they thought the issue of assisted suicide was unimportant. They turned it down because they had already issued two rulings on assisted suicide earlier that same year.

The cases involved challenges to laws against assisted suicide in the states of New York and Washington. The New York case, *Vacco v. Quill*, involved a physician and professor of medicine and psychiatry named Timothy Quill. He was a supporter of physician-assisted suicide who had revealed in 1991 that he had prescribed a lethal dose for a dying patient. Both within and outside the right-to-die movement, many people regarded Quill as a thoughtful and well-qualified spokesman for assisted suicide. Although he had confessed to helping a patient die, he was not seen as a maverick like Jack Kevorkian. Quill believed that assisted suicide should be legalized, but he also argued that it should be carefully regulated, with multiple safeguards against abuse, and should be used only after all other approaches to managing a patient's pain, such as counseling and palliative treatment, had been thoroughly exhausted.

Quill, along with two other doctors and three patients, had filed suit in a federal district court, claiming that a New York State ban on physician-assisted suicide was unconstitutional. Their argument was that the ban violated the constitutional right to personal liberty; they also argued that the ban violated constitutional guarantees of equal treatment for all under the law, because although patients had the legal right to tell their physicians to stop treatment in order to hasten death, they did not have the right to tell physicians to administer treatment to hasten death.

The district court ruled against Quill, who appealed the case to the circuit court. The circuit court ruled in favor of Quill, offering the opinion that there was no constitutional difference between removing a respirator at the request of a patient who was qualified to make that decision and giving a lethal injection or prescription to such a patient. The state appealed this ruling to the U.S. Supreme Court, which agreed to hear the case.

The Court combined *Vacco v. Quill* (Vacco was New York's attorney general) with *Washington v. Glucksberg*, which involved a lawsuit against Washington State's ban on physician-assisted suicide. A doctor named Harold Glucksberg, several other doctors, three terminally ill patients, and a right-to-die organization called Compassion in Dying had argued that the ban was unconstitutional. Under the Fourteenth Amendment of the U.S. Constitution, they claimed, mentally competent adults had the

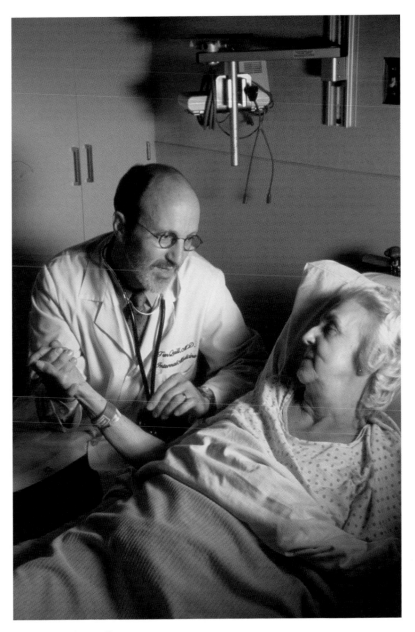

DR. TIMOTHY QUILL WAS A LEADER IN A LOSING BATTLE TO
LEGALIZE PHYSICIAN-ASSISTED SUICIDE IN NEW YORK STATE.

liberty to commit assisted suicide. The district court and then the circuit court agreed with them, ruling the state law unconstitutional. The state appealed the case to the Supreme Court, which heard arguments from both sides in the New York and Washington cases in January 1997. The Court also received briefs, or statements of opinion, on the subject of assisted suicide from a wide range of sources. Arguments against assisted suicide, for example, came from the U.S. government and a group of disabled activists called Not Dead Yet, while others, including the Hemlock Society, submitted briefs in favor of it.

In June 1997 the Court issued its ruling on both cases. By votes of 9 to 0, the justices upheld both states' laws against assisted suicide. The Court ruled that an important distinction exists between withdrawing life support and administering death. The Court had ruled in the *Cruzan* case that a patient had the right to refuse unwanted medical treatment, but that did not mean that the Constitution's guarantees of personal liberty gave the patient a right to die. The Court found no constitutional grounds for a right to physician aid in dying.

The 1997 Supreme Court rulings looked like a crushing defeat for assisted suicide, but few right-to-die supporters had really expected victory. The most interesting aspect of the rulings was that although the votes were unanimous, the justices offered a range of explanations for their decisions. While Justice Stephen Breyer could not include assisted suicide among the fundamental rights guaranteed by the Constitution, he recognized that people have a legitimate desire for "personal control over the manner of death, professional medical assistance, and the avoidance of unnecessary and severe physical suffering." Justice Sandra Day O'Connor quoted an earlier Supreme Court opinion by Justice Louis Brandeis, who said that the task of creating laws to safeguard liberties is "entrusted to the

DISABLED PROTESTORS AGAINST ASSISTED SUICIDE WERE ACTIVE IN THE *QUILL* CASE AND CAME OUT IN FORCE AGAIN IN FAVOR OF THE GOVERNMENT POSITION AGAINST ASSISTED SUICIDE IN *GONZALES V. OREGON*.

'laboratory' of the States." Justice David Souter also pointed out that the state legislatures, rather than the Court, should debate and experiment with solutions to new and important questions such as physician-assisted suicide. In short the Court said that whether to ban or allow physician-assisted suicide was up to the states.

Since the Supreme Court's 1997 ruling, however, no state has legalized physician-assisted suicide. Efforts to pass assisted-suicide laws have failed in more than a dozen states. Hawaii came closest to passing such a law in 2002,

What Do Americans *Really* Think About Assisted Suicide?

The taking of public opinion polls is a highly developed science and art. The science lies in sophisticated statistical formulas that let pollsters make large statements such as "one-third of all Americans believe . . ." after questioning small samples of the population. The art lies in creating the questions. People with strong opinions on an issue usually give consistent responses to questions about that issue, no matter how they are worded. People who are undecided, however, may be affected by changes in the wording of the question, and this can change the overall results of the poll.

Two 2006 polls showed that a majority of Americans support physician-assisted suicide for terminally ill people, but the results of the polls differed significantly. One poll asked: "When a person has a disease that cannot be cured, do you think doctors should be allowed by law to end the patient's life by some painless means if the patient and his family request it?" More than two-thirds of those who answered (69 percent) said yes, 4 percent had no opinion, and slightly more than a quarter (27 percent) said no.

The other poll asked: "If a person has a disease that will

ultimately destroy their mind or body and they want to take their own life, should a doctor be allowed to assist the person in taking their own life, or not?" More than a third of those who answered (37 percent) said no, 7 percent did not answer or said that they did not know, and only 56 percent said yes. What made the difference? More people may have said yes to the first poll because the question included the appealing words *law*, *painless*, and *family*.

The difference is even greater when the emotionally loaded word *suicide* is used. One 2005 poll asked: "Do you think that law should allow doctors to comply with the wishes of a dying patient in severe distress who asks to have his or her life ended, or not?" Only one percent of people said they were not sure, while 29 percent answered no and 70 percent answered yes. This poll indicated strong support for physician aid in dying. But the public was evenly divided when pollsters asked: "In some states, it's legal for doctors to prescribe lethal doses of drugs that a terminally ill patient could use to commit suicide. Do you approve or disapprove of laws that let doctors assist patients who want to end their lives this way?" Nine percent did not know or did not answer, 45 percent disapproved, and 46 percent approved.

Polls about Oregon's Death with Dignity Act have also received widely different responses. One 2005 poll asked: "Under Oregon law, terminally ill adults may request that a physician administer a lethal dose of medication to end their life. Do you agree or disagree with this Oregon law?" Fifty-two percent of the respondents agreed with the law, 41 percent disagreed, and 7 percent did not know.

That same year a different poll asked a longer but more informative question: "There is an Oregon law which allows doctor-assisted suicides for patients with fewer than six months to live. Doctors are allowed to help these patients end their lives, but only if all of the three following conditions are met: the patient requests it three times, there is a second opinion from another doctor and there is a 15-day waiting period for the patient to change his or her mind. Would you favor or oppose such a law in your state?" This time, one percent of respondents did not know or did not answer, 32 percent opposed such a law, and 67 percent favored it. Depending upon which poll they quoted, right-to-life or right-to-die groups could claim that "barely more than half" or "more than two-thirds" of Americans supported Oregon-style physician-assisted suicide.

but the bill fell short of passing by three votes. In Washington State, a former governor named Booth Gardner, ill with Parkinson's disease, has begun a campaign to revive the ballot initiative for assisted suicide in his state. Similar bills have been proposed in California, most recently in 2007, when the proposal was successfully opposed by disability activists and faith-based groups. As of 2007 Oregon was the only state in which physician-assisted suicide was permitted by law.

An overwhelming majority of Americans (84 percent) approve of laws that give terminally ill patients the right to make their own decisions about life-support treatment, but the public is much more evenly divided on the question of assisted suicide for such patients. Forty-six percent of people approve of assisted-suicide laws; 45 percent disapprove. Disapproval is strongest among evangelical or fundamentalist Protestants, Roman Catholics, and conservative Republicans.

On the broader question of whether people have the moral right to end their own lives if they are suffering great pain without hope of improvement, the public is again divided. Overall 60 percent of people say yes, and 34 percent say no. Agreement is highest among people who identify themselves as secular, or nonreligious: 78 percent yes to 20 percent no.

Race is a factor, too. Among whites, 62 percent of people say that people have a moral right to end their suffering, while 31 percent say no. Among blacks 50 percent say no and 43 percent say yes. One explanation for this is that some African Americans may be suspicious of legalized euthanasia, even if it is clearly defined as voluntary. As a group African Americans are less likely to have health insurance than whites, and are more likely to be poor and to have certain health problems, such as AIDS. They may feel themselves to be at special risk if any form of euthanasia becomes legal.

Women, too, may be at special risk, says Susan Wolf, a professor in the University of Minnesota's law and medicine schools and a well-known bioethicist, or specialist in the ethical issues of medicine and biological research. Wolf, who is opposed to assisted suicide, speculates that if voluntary euthanasia is widely legalized, women's traditional role as nurturers of their families may lead them to hasten their own deaths if they think that they have become a burden to their children, or to undervalue their lives if they no longer feel useful.

Whatever the reasons for people's opinions and beliefs about assisted suicide, it is clear that the American public is far from unified on end-of-life issues. This, in turn, suggests that the debate over the right to die will most likely not lead to widespread agreement in the near future.

Around the World

Countries have handled right-to-die issues in a variety of ways. In the majority of nations, euthanasia and assisted suicide are illegal—either they are specifically banned, or they are treated as forms of homicide. In England and Wales, for example, both euthanasia and assisted suicide carry criminal penalties. Scotland, which is also part of the United Kingdom, regards euthanasia as murder but has no laws about assisted suicide, although someone who assisted a suicide might face other criminal charges, such as reckless endangerment of life. Research has shown that physician-assisted suicide and euthanasia do occur in at least some countries where they are outlawed, such as South Africa. Right-to-die movements—as well as the opposing right-to-life movements—are active in some of these nations.

The Netherlands and Belgium are the only countries that have enacted laws to make either euthanasia or physician-

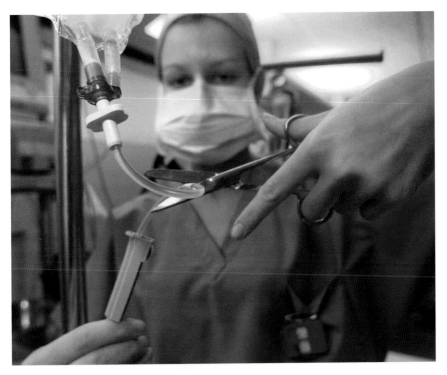

A **BELGIAN HOSPITAL WORKER PREPARES TO CUT A PATIENT'S LIFE-SUPPORT TUBE. IN BELGIUM, PATIENTS HAVE THE LEGAL RIGHT TO DO MORE THAN REFUSE LIFE SUPPORT. THEY MAY ALSO REQUEST PHYSICIAN-ASSISTED SUICIDE.**

assisted suicide legal. Switzerland is a unique case. A 1942 law defined assisting a suicide as illegal only if the assister has selfish motives, such as the desire to gain an inheritance or to be relieved of caretaking duties. The person who assists a suicide does not have to be a physician, and non-Swiss citizens can seek suicide assistance in the country. Since the 1980s nongovernmental organizations such as Dignitas have provided this service.

Many countries have created legal gray areas in which euthanasia and assisted suicide are not permitted by law but are tolerated as a result of court decisions or general agreement. In Japan, for example, a 1962 court ruling on passive euthanasia and a 1995 ruling on active euthanasia allow doctors to perform these acts on terminally ill patients, as long as guidelines about consent are followed. The Scandinavian nations have not legalized aid in dying, but, depending upon the circumstances, authorities may choose not to prosecute physicians who perform the acts. When prosecutions do take place, sentences are often light.

The South American nation of Colombia entered the gray area in 1997, when the country's highest court ruled in a 6-to-3 decision that individuals have the right to end their lives and that physicians cannot be prosecuted for helping them. The court also encouraged the Colombian Congress to pass a law that would govern the practices of assisted suicide and euthanasia, but this has not happened. A 2005 bill failed to gather support among lawmakers, most likely because lawmakers hesitate to stir up religious opposition in the predominantly Roman Catholic nation. As a result assisted suicide and euthanasia are private matters between patients and physicians in Colombia, with no formal guidelines or record-keeping.

Physician-assisted suicide became legal—briefly—in part of Australia in the mid–1990s. In 1995 the legislature of the Northern Territories, Australia's least-populated region, passed the Rights of the Terminally Ill Act by a vote of 15 to 10. This law was similar to Oregon's Death with Dignity Act (which had already been passed but had not yet gone into effect). Unlike the Oregon law, the Australian law required the assisting physician to be present at the patient's death, although the patient had to perform the final act.

The highly controversial law went into effect on July 1, 1996, but only one physician in the territory declared openly that he was willing to assist suicides. He was a right-to-die activist named Dr. Philip Nitschke who, like Dr. Kevorkian, designed a device that would administer a lethal injection. To activate the injection the patient had to use a keyboard to complete a three-stage consent.

Almost as soon as the law went into effect, its days were numbered. Australia's national parliament can override laws passed by the country's territories (although not by its states), and various groups that opposed the law lobbied the country's legislature to repeal it. Some of the opponents belonged to religious or right-to-life organizations. Others were activists for the Aborigines, Australia's native people, who make up more than a quarter of the population of the Northern Territories. Some Aborigines had expressed fears that the new law could be used against them without their consent if they went into hospitals, and activists feared that this would make the Aborigines, already a disadvantaged group in the Australian population, less likely to seek health care.

The Australian parliament overturned the Rights of the Terminally Ill Act in March 1997. The law had been in effect for nine months, during which seven people asked Dr. Nitschke to end their lives. He was able to do so for four of them before the law was repealed. Bob Dent, the terminally ill cancer patient who urged the public not to deny him his right to death on his own terms, was the first.

Is there a worldwide trend toward greater acceptance of the right to die and legalization of assisted death? Ian Dowbiggin, a Canadian historian of medicine, thinks not. In *A Concise History of Euthanasia: Life, Death, God, and Medicine* (2005) he points out that support for the right to die has traditionally been highest in the secular nations of the Western world. Some major religions, however, are opposed to euthanasia—Roman Catholicism, Islam, Judaism, and evangelical Protestantism are among them. Conservative or deeply religious members of these faiths are highly likely to oppose the right to die. Their numbers are rising in the Western countries, partly because of immigration and partly because religious conservatives generally have higher birthrates than secular people. At the same time, social history demonstrates that the children and grandchildren of conservative and religious parents often shift toward more liberal and secular values. The combination of these trends may keep alive the debate over the right to die for some time.

5
For and Against
Aid in Dying

When a New York psychotherapist named Sandra Weiner learned in 1987 that her breast cancer had returned and had invaded her lungs and bones, she obtained prescriptions for pain and sleeping pills from her physician. Although neither she nor her doctor spoke of it directly, both knew what Weiner intended to do. Weiner filled the prescriptions and kept the medications on hand. By 1990 a tumor was forming in her throat. Realizing that she would soon be unable to swallow, she wrote a letter to friends, then drank a cup of tea in which her daughter had dissolved the pills, at her request.

"I wanted to go peacefully feeling well—living life on my terms to the end," Weiner had written. "Not dying in a hospital, sick and emaciated on god-forbid a series of tubes and a respirator. . . . Anyway, I made my choices. I had superb medical physicians. I was loved and cared for. I have no regrets." Said her daughter, "She just slipped away. It all went very smoothly, exactly as she wanted it. I saw that as a gift from God."

Some people would agree that Weiner's peaceful death on her own terms was a gift from God. Many would not. Religious believers, like the general population, are divided on the question of whether it is ever right to end one's own life, even to escape suffering, terminal illness, or an unwanted, undignified form of death. But although there have always been many believers among people who support the right to die, religious belief is a powerful motivation for many of those who oppose that right, just as it is for many members of the antiabortion movement. To them, the giving and taking of life belong to God.

Opinions based on religious belief—or the lack of it—seldom give way to rational arguments from the opposite position. Either the belief is there or it is not. Where the issue of the right to die is concerned, however, perhaps each side would do well to ponder one question from the other side. Believers could ask themselves: Should religious opposition to the right to die be permitted to affect the lives of competent adults who do not share the religious belief? And nonbelievers could ask themselves: Should the notion of the sanctity, or sacredness, of life—a notion that underlies much of modern law and culture—be disregarded because it is rooted in religion?

There are many other grounds on which to evaluate the right to die. Books, articles, and Internet sites by the thousands discuss the arguments for and against assisted suicide and euthanasia. Some of the most important arguments appear again and again in these discussions. They have helped shape opinions, policies, and laws about physician-assisted suicide and voluntary euthanasia.

The Physician's Role

The Hippocratic Oath is a statement that has been credited to Hippocrates, a Greek physician of the fourth

THE HIPPOCRATIC OATH, CREDITED TO THE GREEK PHYSICIAN HIPPOCRATES, IS OFTEN USED IN ARGUMENTS AGAINST PHYSICIAN-ASSISTED SUICIDE OR EUTHANASIA.

century BCE, although the origin and exact wording of the oath are uncertain. The oath declares that the physician's prime duty is to do no harm. It contains a specific ban on helping patients die. In one common version of the oath, that ban reads: "To please no one will I prescribe a deadly drug, nor give advice which may cause his death." It has been traditional for many new doctors to recite the Hippocratic Oath at their graduation ceremonies.

Opponents of assisted dying regard the Hippocratic Oath as the ultimate expression of a doctor's role and duty—and a reason why physicians should not help patients die. Not all physicians take the oath, however, and it has no legal force. For hundreds of years physicians have been redefining their roles, just as religious beliefs have shifted away from Apollo and the other ancient Greek deities mentioned in the Hippocratic Oath.

Other questions about the physician's role in dying are more significant. Many physicians have profound professional or personal objections to helping people die. The vast majority of right-to-die supporters agree that no law should require any physician to perform assisted suicide or euthanasia. Participation in such actions should be strictly voluntary; at most, physicians who disagree with their patients' choices should be required to refer them to other doctors. At the same time physicians who do exercise a legal right to help their patients die should not experience prejudice or setbacks within their profession.

The relationship between patients and physicians is an important issue. Opponents to the right to die have objected that if euthanasia becomes legal, patients—especially old, sick, and vulnerable people who may be socially isolated and have no supportive family members—may fear that their physicians will pressure them to choose death. This could erode the trust that patients should be able to feel toward their physicians.

The strongest safeguard against this danger is commu-

nication. Patients and physicians alike should be well informed about patient rights under aid-in-dying laws as
well as in other areas of care; such laws should include
mechanisms, such as ombudsmen or review boards, to
which patients or their families can report any concern.
Supporters of aid in dying point out that patients also need
to be able to trust their physicians to listen to their thoughts
on end-of-life issues and to respect their decisions.

The Risk of Abuse

There have been well-documented cases of non-voluntary
euthanasia in which doctors and nurses have killed people
without their permission—sometimes without any reason
to think they would ever give permission. Such tragic cases
are recognized as being outside the law. If the line between
helping patients and killing them is deliberately erased,
however, what is to prevent physicians' rights to kill their
patients from being abused? Abuse could range from the
actual killing of patients without permission to more sub-
tle forms, such as using misinformation or psychological
pressure to push difficult or unprofitable patients toward
choosing death. Economic abuse could occur when families urge patients to die because of the cost of health care,
or when HMOs and insurance companies pressure doctors
and patients to choose death over continued medical
expenses.

Potential solutions to these concerns include watchdog
groups or review boards; safeguards such as requiring
meetings with more than one physician before a request to
die can be granted; and a full and public reporting process,
similar to that used in Oregon, that includes detailed information about patients who take advantage of assisted
suicide laws—not their names, but statistics about age,
race, level of education, and medical condition. Anyone
who is interested should have access to the records.

Patients who are vulnerable to abuse—perhaps confused about their own medical conditions, suffering from depression, or worried about medical bills—might seek aid in dying whether or not such aid were legal. If so they would certainly be safer in a carefully overseen, regulated system than in the hands of maverick "independent operators" such as Dr. Kevorkian or people passing out suicide advice on the Internet.

The Slippery Slope

Picture yourself standing at the top of a slope of some slippery substance—glass, maybe, or mud. You intend to take just one step, but the slope is so steep and so slippery that you can't stop. Pretty soon you are stumbling downhill, faster and faster.

The slippery slope is a good metaphor for a process that starts small but soon gets out of hand. It is often used as a warning against something that looks reasonable but could lead irresistibly to other, more questionable things. Opponents of assisted suicide fear that legalizing voluntary death for the terminally ill will lead to "death on demand" for other groups of people: those who are sick but not dying, those who are depressed or mentally ill, the disabled, people confined to nursing homes, those who are simply unhappy or bored with life, perhaps even the young. If it is tragic when such people seek suicide on their own, should society sanction or assist their deaths?

A few spokespeople for the movement have said that they would like to see the right to die extended to the disabled or even to any competent adults. These are minority views, however. Public opinion polls and published writings on the subject consistently lean toward strict limits on the right to choose assisted dying, as well as strict controls on the process. And while many disabled people and their advocates oppose assisted dying on the grounds that there may be pressure for them to end their lives, some disabled people disagree. They deny a need for extra protection, arguing that people who are mentally competent but physically disabled have the same abilities to weigh alternatives and make decisions as everyone else.

The slippery slope has been used to argue against all kinds of things, from integrated schools and voting rights for teenagers to interracial and gay marriage. Some of those things became legal; some did not. Citizens and lawmakers have always found it possible to take a single step and then stop. All that is necessary is that the law serve as a handrail. Americans made the choice to give women the vote, for example, but have drawn the line at lowering the voting age to sixteen or even fourteen, as has been suggested in some states.

When it comes to evaluating the risks of a slippery slope for assisted dying, citizens and lawmakers will be better served by evidence than by speculation about possible future problems. So far The Netherlands and Oregon are the world's laboratories, where experiments with legalized aid in dying are under way. As is often the case, however, the early statistics from these experiments can be interpreted in more than one way. To people who are opposed to assisted dying, even one questionable death, one documented case of involuntary euthanasia, is too much. To those who believe that society should find a way to help terminally ill people end their lives with medical aid, on the other hand, the percentage of questionable deaths is very small, and the solution lies not in denying people the right to die but in taking greater care to ensure that it is properly carried out.

Alternatives to Death

Many critics and supporters of assisted dying agree on one thing: better end-of-life care is needed. Hospice services, better use of pain medication, counseling, therapy to combat depression, massage therapy, aid to caregivers, and other kinds of palliative care can do a great deal to comfort patients who are incurably or terminally ill. The less fear people have of uncontrollable pain, humiliation, or indignity in the last stage of life, the less likely they are to consider suicide or euthanasia a desirable option.

One encouraging sign for everyone who cares about the welfare of such patients—or anyone who wonders

HOSPICE CARE HAS BEEN GREATLY ON THE RISE IN THE UNITED STATES; IT IS A WAY TO MAKE A DYING PATIENT AS COMFORTABLE AS POSSIBLE. DYING PATIENTS SUCH AS LENA CHRISTENSEN, AGE 104, WERE EVACUATED ALONG WITH OTHERS IN THE AFTERMATH OF HURRICANE KATRINA, AND CARED FOR BY NURSES SUCH AS SHIRLEY HULGAN.

what his or her own last days might be like—is the recent rise of interest in palliative care in the medical profession, and the increase in palliative care available to patients. Physician Diane E. Meier, director of a palliative care center at Mount Sinai Hospital in New York, reported in 2004 on the growth of in-hospital palliative care programs: "In almost 1,100 American hospitals, a palliative care program is now standard practice; this number has grown more than 63 percent since 2000. . . . In addition, more than 320 primary care residency programs now offer palliative medicine as part of their curricula, and a national effort has been mounted to recognize palliative medicine as a medical subspecialty." If such services to hospital patients continue to increase, along with hospice programs and pain-management programs to help patients who are living at home, the number of people who are driven to hasten their deaths may remain small.

The Value of Life

The views of many who oppose euthanasia and physician-assisted dying are based on something that is both real and hard to define: the value of life. No sane person would deny that life, in general, is precious and should be valued over death. Making death available as a choice, in this view, demeans and devalues life. From this perspective, upholding the value of life is not just a personal choice. It is a social and ethical responsibility. Attorney and right-to-life advocate Wesley J. Smith has said, "The equality-of-human-life ethic requires that each of us be considered of equal inherent worth, and it makes the preservation and protection of human life society's first priority. Accepting euthanasia would replace the equality-of-human-life ethic with a utilitarian and nihilistic 'death culture' that views the intentional ending of certain human lives as an appropriate and necessary answer to life's most difficult challenges."

Although the value of *life* is something few would deny, perhaps the value of *a life* can only be defined by the person who is living it. "The greatest human freedom is to live, and die, according to one's own desires and beliefs," says the organization Death with Dignity. If society gives people the right to worship and live as they please, as long as they do not harm others, should not people also have the right to die as they please, at least under certain circumstances? When the joy of life is overcome by pain and helplessness, perhaps it is the individual's right to say, "I value what my life has been, and now I choose to end it." Which of these two positions the law will support in years to come depends on all of us.

Notes

Chapter 1

p. 10, par. 2, Joni Eareckson Tada, in an interview titled "Notes in the Key of Life," February 3, 2005, http://cindy swanslife.blogspot.com/2005/02/my-interview-with-joni-eareckson-tada.html

p. 12, par. 1, Joni Eareckson Tada, *When Is It Right to Die?* Grand Rapids, MI: Zondervan, 1992, p. 25.

p. 12, par. 1, Tada, p. 25.

p. 12, pars. 3–5, Tada, p. 169.

p. 13, par. 2, Tada, p. 20.

p. 14, par. 1, Tada, p. 180.

p. 16, par. 3, Dennis McClellan, "Interview with Dax Cowart, J.D.," in Robert C. Horn III, *Who's Right? Whose Right? Seeking Answers and Dignity in the Debate Over the Right to Die.* Sanford, FL: DC Press, 2001, p. 97.

p. 17, par. 1, McClellan, p. 102.

p. 17, par. 3, McClellan, p. 105.

p. 17, par. 3, McClellan, p. 104.

p. 18, par. 2, McClellan, p. 103.

p. 18, par. 3, McClellan, p. 109.

p. 19, par. 4, Sue Woodman, *Last Rights: The Struggle Over the Right to Die.* New York: Plenum, 1998, p. 8.

p. 20, par. 2, Woodman, p. 9.

p. 20, par. 3, Woodman, p. 13.
p. 21, par. 1, Woodman, p. 261.
p. 21, par. 1 Woodman, p. 262.
p. 21, par. 2, Woodman, pp. 262–263.
p. 21, par. 3, Woodman, p. 263.
p. 25, par. 4, All Svart quotations are from Don Colburn, "She chose it all on the day she died," *Oregonian*, September 30, 2007, pp. A1, A12–A13.

Chapter 2
p. 30, par. 1, Georges Minois, *History of Suicide: Voluntary Death in Western Culture*, trans. Lydia Cochrane. Baltimore: Johns Hopkins University Press, 1999, p. 43.
p. 30, par. 1, Minois, p. 47.
p. 30, par. 3, Quoted in A. Alvarez, "The History of Suicide," in Michael M. Uhlmann, ed. *Last Rights? Assisted Suicide and Euthanasia Debated*. Washington, DC: Ethics and Public Policy Center, 1998, p. 65.
p. 32, par. 2, Minois, p. 45.
p. 32, par. 3, Minois, p. 44.
p. 34, par. 3, Minois, p. 51.
p. 34, par. 5–p. 35, par. 1, Minois, p. 52.
p. 35, par. 3, Byron L. Sherwin, "Jewish Views on Euthanasia," in Michael M. Uhlmann, ed. *Last Rights? Assisted Suicide and Euthanasia Debated*. Washington, DC: Ethics and Public Policy Center, 1998, p. 155.
p. 36, par. 2, Minois, p. 26.
p. 38, par. 4–p. 39, par. 1, Thomas More, *Utopia*, in *The Complete Works of St. Thomas More*, Edward Surtz and J.H. Hexter, editors. New Haven, CT: Yale University Press, 1965, Vol. 4, p. 187.
p. 39, par. 3, Michael M. Uhlmann, "Western Thought on Suicide from Plato to Kant," in Michael M. Uhlmann, ed. *Last Rights? Assisted Suicide and Euthanasia Debated*. Washington, DC: Ethics and Public Policy Center, 1998, p. 11.
p. 39, par. 4, Minois, p. 67.
p. 39, par. 4, Minois, p. 67.
p. 41, par. 1, Quoted in Minois, p. 91.
p. 41, par. 1, Quoted in Minois, pp. 91–92.
p. 42, par. 3, Quoted in Minois, p. 251.

p. 43, par. 2, Minois, p. 236.

p. 44, par. 2, According to the National Center for Health Statistics, maintained by the Centers for Disease Control and Prevention, of the 2,401,400 people who died in the United States in 2004 (the most recent year for which figures were available), nearly 1 million were hospital patients; nearly 180,000 were being treated as outpatients or in emergency rooms; more than 530,000 were in nursing homes or other long-term care facilities; 10,000 were in hospices; and almost 587,000 died at home. Data available online at http://www.cdc.gov/nchs/data/dvs/MortFinal 2004_Worktable309.pdf

p. 44, par. 3, Quoted in Peter Filene, *In the Arms of Others: A Cultural History of the Right-to-Die in America*. Chicago: Dee, 1998, p. 4.

p. 46, par. 4 and p. 48, par. 1, Filene, p. 6.

p. 48, par. 5 and p. 49, par. 1, Ian Dowbiggin, *A Concise History of Euthanasia: Life, Death, God, and Medicine*. Lanham, MD: Rowman & Littlefield, 2005, p. 73.

p. 49, par. 2, Quoted in Dowbiggin, p. 74.

p. 50, par. 2, Quoted in Filene, p. 6.

p. 50, par. 4, Quoted in Filene, p. 8.

p. 50, par. 4, "The Right to Die," *Time*, January 9, 1956, p. 62.

Chapter 3

p. 52, par. 1, Quoted in M. L. Tina Stevens, "What Quinlan Can Tell Kevorkian About the Right to Die," *Humanist*, March/April 1997, http://findarticles.com/p/articles/mi_m 1374/is_n2_v57/ai_19217209/

p. 52, par. 3–p. 53, par. 1, Quoted in Stevens, http://findarticles.com/p/articles/mi_m1374/is_n2_v57/ai_19217209/

p. 55, pars. 3–4, Quoted in Peter Filene, *In the Arms of Others: A Cultural History of the Right-to-Die in America*. Chicago: Dee, 1998, p. 48.

p. 56, par. 3, Quoted in Filene, p. 216.

p. 59, par. 4, Filene, p. 216.

p. 59, par. 4–p. 60, par. 1, Ian Dowbiggin, *A Concise History of Euthanasia: Life, Death, God, and Medicine*. Lanham, MD: Rowman & Littlefield, 2005, p. 112.

p. 62, par. 2, Barry Rosenfeld, *Assisted Suicide and the Right to Die: The Interface of Social Science, Public Policy, and*

Medical Ethics. Washington, DC: American Psychological Association, 2004, p. 45.

p. 65, par. 1, Derek Humphry, "The Case for Rational Suicide," in Michael M. Uhlmann, editor, *Last Rights? Assisted Suicide and Euthanasia Debated.* Washington, DC: Ethics and Public Policy Center, 1998, pp. 307–308.

p. 68, par. 1, *Cruzan v. Director, Missouri Department of Health,* 497 U.S. 261 (1990), http://caselaw.lp.findlaw.com/scripts/getcase.pl?court=us&vol=497&invol=261

p. 68, par. 2, *Cruzan v. Director, Missouri Department of Health,* 497 U.S. 261 (1990).

p. 75, par. 3, Dowbiggin, p. 74.

Chapter 4

p. 78, par. 3, Barry Rosenfeld, *Assisted Suicide and the Right to Die: The Interface of Social Science, Public Policy, and Medical Ethics.* Washington, DC: American Psychological Association, 2004, p. 133.

p. 79, par. 4, Anthony Deutsch for Associated Press, "Dutch Law Ends Euthanasia Debate," April 11, 2001, http://www.wwrn.org/article.php?idd=14663&sec=36&con=45

p. 79, par. 5, Deutsch, http://www.wwrn.org/article.php?idd=14663&sec=36&con=45

p. 80, par. 1, Deutsch, http://www.wwrn.org/article.php?idd=14663&sec=36&con=45

p. 80, par. 2, Herbert Hendin, "The Dutch Experience," in Michael M. Uhlmann, ed. *Last Rights? Assisted Suicide and Euthanasia Debated.* Washington, DC: Ethics and Public Policy Center, 1998, pp. 367–369; reprinted from *Suicide in America,* 3rd edition, 1998.

p. 80, par. 3, Quoted in Paul Wilkes, "The Next Pro-Lifers," *New York Times Magazine,* July 21, 1996, p. 26.

p. 81, par. 1, Amanda Gardner, "Dutch Euthanasia Rates Steady After Legalization," U.S. Department of Health and Human Services, healthfinder.gov, http://www.healthfinder.gov/news/newsstory.asp?docID=604457

p. 81, par. 3, Hendin, p. 380.

p. 82, par. 2, Rosenfeld, p. 39.

p. 83, par. 2–p. 84, par. 1, Peter Filene, *In the Arms of Others: A Cultural History of the Right-to-Die in America.* Chicago: Dee, 1998, p. 200.

p. 85, par. 2, All DWDA figures from "Death With Dignity Act, 2006 Annual Report," Oregon Department of Human Services, http://www.oregon.gov/DHS/ph/pas/

p. 88, par. 3, Quoted in Filene, p. 199.

p. 88, par. 3–p. 89, par. 1, Quoted in Rosenfeld, p. 38.

pp. 90–92, Questions and response data for all polls from "Right to Die: Red Flags," Public Agenda, http://www.publicagenda.org/issues/red_flags.cfm?issue_type=right2die

p. 93, par. 2, All figures from "Strong Public Support for Right to Die," Pew Research Center, January 5, 2006, http://people-press.org/reports/display.php3?ReportID=266

p. 93, par. 4, All figures from "Strong Public Support for Right to Die," Pew Research Center, January 5, 2006, http://people-press.org/reports/display.php3?ReportID=266

p. 93, par. 4, Ian Dowbiggin, *A Concise History of Euthanasia: Life, Death, God, and Medicine.* Lanham, MD: Rowman & Littlefield, 2005, p. 151.

p. 96, par. 2, Associated Press, "Euthanasia Regularly Practiced in Colombia," July 31, 2005, http://www.msnbc.msn.com/id/8778072/

Chapter 5

p. 99, par. 2, Letter and quotation from Sue Woodman, *Last Rights: The Struggle Over the Right to Die.* New York: Plenum, 1998, pp. 44–45.

p. 107, par. 2, Diane E. Meier, "Reducing Costs, Improving Lives, with Palliative Care," Hospitals and Health Networks, http://www.hhnmag.com/hhnmag_app/hospitalcon nect/search/article.jsp?dcrpath=HHNMAG/PubsNewsArticle/data/041026HHN_Online_MeierMD&domain=HHNMAG

p. 107, par, 3–p. 108, par. 1, Wesley J. Smith, Introduction, *Forced Exit*, 1997, http://www.euthanasiaprocon.org/top 10.html

p. 108, par. 2, "Who We Are," Death with Dignity National Center, http://www.deathwithdignity.org

Further Information

Further Reading

Altman, Linda J. *Death: An Introduction to Medical-Ethical Dilemmas*. Berkeley Heights, NJ: Enslow Publishers, 2000.

Balkin, Karen F., ed. *Assisted Suicide*. Detroit: Greenhaven, 2005.

Cavan, Seamus, and Sean Dolan. *Euthanasia: Debate Over the Right to Die*. New York: Rosen, 2000.

Egendorf, Laura, editor. *Assisted Suicide*. San Diego: Greenhaven, 1998.

Ferguson, John E., Jr. *The Right to Die*. New York: Chelsea House, 2007.

Haley, James, ed. *Death and Dying: Opposing Viewpoints*. San Diego: Greenhaven, 2003.

Rebman, Renee. *Euthanasia and the "Right to Die."* Berkeley Heights, NJ: Enslow Publishers, 2002.

Yount, Lisa. *Right to Die and Euthanasia*. New York: Facts On File, 2007.

Web Sites

http://www.bbc.co.uk/religion/ethics/euthanasia/against/agai
nst_1.shtml
A companion to the British Broadcasting Corporation's Religion and Ethics series, this page presents a detailed overview of religious, ethical, practical, and historical arguments against euthanasia.

http://www.deathreference.com
The online Encyclopedia of Death and Dying offers brief, nonpartisan articles on topics such as end-of-life issues and euthanasia.

http://www.deathwithdignity.org
The Web site of the Death with Dignity National Center supports right-to-die legislation and the option of voluntary euthanasia for the terminally ill.

http://estate.findlaw.com/estate-planning/living-wills/estate-planning-law-state-living-wills.html
Findlaw, a site devoted to legal information, maintains a list of the rules governing living wills and other advance health care directives in all states and the District of Columbia.

http://www.euthanasia.com
Euthanasia.com is opposed to voluntary euthanasia and assisted suicide. Its Web site presents an international collection of articles in support of that position, from personal stories to legal and medical perspectives.

http://www.euthanasiaprocon.org
Starting with the question "Should euthanasia be legal?" Euthanasia ProCon promotes a balanced discussion of end-of-life issues, with viewpoints from individuals and groups on both sides of the right-to-die question.

http://www.finalexit.org
The Web site of the Euthanasia Research and Guidance Organization is also the site of Derek Humphry, founder of the

Hemlock Society; it has links to many essays, articles, and resources that support the right to die.

http://www.hli.org
Human Life International is an organization that supports life and opposes both abortion and euthanasia based on religious principles.

http://www.nrlc.org
The National Right to Life Committee opposes euthanasia as well as abortion; its Web site includes overviews of euthanasia issues, as well as information about euthanasia alternatives such as the Will to Live.

http://www.oregon.gov/DHS/ph/pas/
The state of Oregon's Department of Health and Human Services maintains this Web site, which contains the annual reports on the use of the Death with Dignity Act, the only physician-assisted suicide law in the United States.

http://www.pccef.org
Physicians for Compassionate Care Education Foundation is an organization of medical professionals who are opposed to physician-assisted suicide; its Web site offers links to articles and video presentations on the topic.

http://www.publicagenda.org/issues/frontdoor.cfm?issue_type =right2die
The nonpartisan organization Public Agenda maintains this site, which offers an overview of right-to-die issues and legislation, perspectives from both sides, and resources for more information.

http://www.worldrtd.net/
The World Federation of Right to Die Societies is a link to thirty-eight organizations (from twenty-three countries) that support right-to-die legislation.

Bibliography

Cohen-Almagor, Raphael. *The Right to Die with Dignity: An Argument in Medicine, Ethics, and Law*. Piscataway, NJ: Rutgers University Press, 2001.

Colby, William. *Long Goodbye: The Deaths of Nancy Cruzan*. Carlsbad, CA: Hay House, 2002.

Dowbiggin, Ian. *A Concise History of Euthanasia: Life, Death, God, and Medicine*. Lanham, MD: Rowman & Littlefield, 2005.

Filene, Peter G. *In the Arms of Others: A Cultural History of the Right-to-Die in America*. Chicago: Dee, 1998.

Horn, Robert C. III. *Who's Right? Whose Right? Seeking Answers and Dignity in the Debate Over the Right to Die*. Sanford, FL: DC Press, 2001.

Lader, Lawrence. *Ideas Triumphant*. Santa Ana, CA: Seven Locks, 2003.

Minois, Georges. *History of Suicide: Voluntary Death in Western Culture.* Translated by Lydia G. Cochrane. Baltimore: Johns Hopkins University Press, 1999.

Nicol, Neal, and Harry Wylie. *Between the Dying and the Dead: Dr. Jack Kevorkian's Life and the Battle to Legalize Euthanasia.* Madison: University of Wisconsin Press, 2006.

Rosenfeld, Barry. *Assisted Suicide and the Right to Die: The Interface of Social Science, Public Policy, and Medical Ethics.* Washington, DC: American Psychological Association, 2004.

Tada, Joni Eareckson. *When Is It Right to Die? Suicide, Euthanasia, Suffering, Mercy.* Grand Rapids, MI: Zondervan, 1992.

Uhlmann, Michael M., ed. *Last Right? Assisted Suicide and Euthanasia Debated.* Washington, DC: Ethics and Public Policy Center, 1998.

Woodman, Sue. *Last Rights: The Struggle Over the Right to Die.* New York: Plenum, 1998.

Zucker, Marjorie B., ed. *The Right to Die Debate: A Documentary History.* Westport, CT: Greenwood, 1999.

Index

Page numbers in **boldface** are illustrations, tables, and charts.

Aborigines, 97
abortion issues, 66, 100
abuse risk, 23, 81, 86, 93–94,
    97, 103–104
acceptance stage of grief, **57**, **83**
active euthanasia, 45, 46, 53,
    63, 64, 81, 96
Adkins, Janet, 72
advance directives, 23, 60–63,
    67
    defined, 22, 60
African Americans, 93–94
AIDS, 93
Alzheimer's disease, 72
American Catholic Church, **54**
American College of Surgeons,
    52
American Medical Association
    (AMA), 56
American Psychiatric
    Association, 50
amyotrophic lateral sclerosis
    (ALS), 73
anger stage of grief, **57**
antibiotics, 51
antisuicide laws, 40
Aquinas, Thomas, 37
Aristotle, 33, 37

artificial nutrition and
    hydration (ANH), 22–23
    Karen Ann Quinlan, 58,
        59, 61
    Nancy Cruzan, 67, 68, 69
    Terri Schiavo, 69, 70, 75
Ashcroft, John, **83**, 84
assisted suicide, 8–9, 15, 30–31,
    38, 50, 53, 60. *See also*
    Physician-assisted suicide.
    disabled and, **11**, 13, 15,
        88, 89, 104–105
    DWDA (Oregon), 82–85,
        83
    internationally, 94–98
    Jack Kevorkian and, 72–74
    laws against, 64, 75
    legalization question, 18,
        30, **65**
    Netherlands' toleration of,
        78–81
    pro/con debate, 100–108
    U.S. Supreme Court on,
        85–89, **87**, **89**, 93–94
Athens city-state, 30, 31, 64
Augustine of Hippo, 36, 37
Australia, Northern Territory,
    96–97

Baby Doe case, 49
ballot initiative, 82
Ballot Measure 16, 82
Ballot Measure 51, 83, 84
bargaining stage of grief, 57
Belgium, 79, 95, **95**
Biathanatos, 41
Bible, 41
Bollinger, Allan, 49
Borst, Els, 79
*Boston Medical and Surgical
    Journal*, 46
Brandeis, Louis, 88
Breyer, Stephen, 88
British Voluntary Euthanasia
    Society, 46
burn victims, 16, 17
Bush, George W., 70, 75
Bush, Jeb, 70

cancer, 15, 25, 50, 55, 64, 77,
    85, 97, 99
carbon monoxide, 73
cardiopulmonary resuscitation
    (CPR), 62
caregivers, aid to, 106
care institutions, 62
Cartier, Dr., 55
Cato, 34
child abuse, 49
Christ, Jesus, 36
Christensen, Lena, **106**
Christianity, 13, 15, 36–37, 40,
    41
Colombia, 96
coma, 7, 14–15, 27, 50, 57–59,
    69
comfort care, 24, 56, 60
Compassion & Choices of
    Oregon, 27
Compassion in Dying, 86
competence, issue of, 14, 17–18,
    22–23, 58–61, 68, 86, 100, 105

Controlled Substance Act
    (CSA), 84
counseling, access to, 18, 24,
    56, 86, 106
Cowart, Dax, 16, 17, 18
Cruzan, Joe, 67
Cruzan, Joyce, 67
Cruzan, Nancy, 67–70, 75
*Cruzan v. Director, Missouri
    Department of Health*, 68,
    88
Cry for Life, 80

Darrow, Clarence, 49
David, Jacques Louis, 31
death, 7
    alternatives to, 106–107
    attitudes about, 10
    as political issue, 7, 70, 75
    as social issue, 7, 19, 37, 75
    as taboo subject, 55
deathbed decisions, 61
"death culture," 108
"death on demand," 104
Death with Dignity, 108
Debs, Eugene V., 49
denial stage of grief, **57, 83**
Dent, Bob, 77, 97
depression, 14, 17, 20–21, 63,
    73, 80, 104, 106
depression stage of grief, **57**
dialysis machine, 61
Dignitas, 95
dignity, die with, 27, 107
    modern medicine versus,
    52–53
    in Oregon, 82–85
disabled, **11**, 13, 15, 104–105
    activists, 88, **89**
Doctor Death, 72–74
Donne, John, 41
"Do Not Resuscitate" (DNR)
    order, 22, 62

double effect, 23, 45, 53, 81
Dowbiggin, Ian, 97
durable power of attorney for
  health care, 22, 23, 61, 62
Dutch Royal Medical Society,
  79
Dutch Supreme Court, 79, 80
dystopia, 38

Eareckson, Joni, 10, **11**, 12–15
economic abuse, 103
Eighmey, George, 27
the Enlightenment, 41–43
Epicureans, 32
equality-of-human-life ethic,
  107–108
equal treatment under law, 86
Ethics, 33
ethics, 9, 94, 107–108
eugenics, 48, 49, 50
euthanasia, 13, 15, 58–59, 66,
  80
  active, 45–46, 53, 63–64,
    81, 96
  defined, 23, 44
  historically, 29, 35, 37,
    38–39
  internationally, 94–98
  involuntary, 23, 105
  Jack Kevorkian and, 72–74
  legislation, 8, 46, 49, 64,
    93–94
  modern nightmares, 48–51
  and Nazi eugenics, 50
  Netherlands' toleration of,
    79–81
  non-voluntary, 23, 81, 103
  passive, 45, 53, 96
  pro/con debate, 100–108
  religious opposition to,
    97–98
  voluntary, 8–9, 14–15, 23,
    29, 38, 40, 46, 50, 60,

    64, 72, 74, 77, 79–81,
    93–94, 104
Euthanasia Research and Guidance
  Organization (ERGO), 66
euthanasia societies, 46, **47**, 50,
  64, 66
Euthanasia Society of America
  (ESA), 46, 50, 64
evangelical Protestants, 93, 96
extermination, 48

Farrell, John, 52
felony, suicide as, 63
five stages of grief, 57, **83**
France, 63
French Revolution, 63

Gallup Poll, 46
Gardner, Booth, 93
Glucksberg, Harold, 86
Gonzales, Alberto, 84
Gonzales v. *Oregon*, 84, **89**
"good breeding/bad breeding,"
  48
the good death, 43–46, 48
Greeks, 30–32, **31**, 34, 35, 37

Haiselden, Harry, 49
health care decisions, 70, 103
  advance directives for,
    60–61, 67
  for incompetent/no written
    guidelines, 70
health care proxy, 61, 62, 63
health insurance, 93, 103
health management
  organizations (HMOs), 62,
    103
hemlock poisoning, 30, 31, **31**
Hemlock Society, 64–66, **65**, 88
Hendin, Herbert, 80, 81
heroic martyrdom, 36
Hippocrates, 100, **101**

Hippocratic Oath, 100, **101**, 102
Holocaust, 48, 49, 50
homosexuals, 48
Horace, 39
hospice, 24, 59, 73, 106–107, **106**
  defined, 23
  movement in America, 57, 59–60
  philosophy, 60
  purpose of, 56
hospitals
  advance directives and, 62
  in-hospital palliative care, 107
Hulgan, Shirley, **106**
Hume, David, 41, 42, 43
Humphry, Derek, 64, 65, 66
Hurricane Katrina, **106**
Huurman, Piet, 80

incompetence, 70, 81
incurable illness, 13, 15, 23, 106
  euthanasia, 46
  suicide, 24, 29, 32, 38, 41
individual rights, 16–19, 42–43, 64
informed choice, 18, 22, 56, 62, 103
insanity, suicide and, 37, 40, 63
institutionalization, 49
International Congress of Anesthesiology, 53
Internet, 27–28, 100, 104
involuntary euthanasia, 23, 105

Japan, 96
John Paul II, Roman Catholic Pope, 53, 70
Joni and Friends, 13
Josephus, 36
Judaism, 97
  ancient views on suicide, 30, 35–36
Holocaust, 48–49, 50
"justifiable suicide," 65

Kant, Immanuel, 42, 43
Karen Ann Quinlan Center of Hope, 59
Keller, Helen, 49
Kennedy, Foster, 50
Kevorkian, Jack, 72–74, 86, 97, 104
Kübler-Ross, Elisabeth, 56, 57, **83**

Laertius, Diogenes, 32
Laws, 33
laws, 29
  aid in dying, 103
  antisuicide, 40, 63, 64
  concerning assisted suicide, 18, 30, 64, 72, 77, 79, 93, 105
  concerning euthanasia, 8, 46, 49, 64, 72, 79–81
  concerning suicide, 30, 40, 42–43, 63
  life support, 49, 61, 93
  supporting living wills, 61, 63
  supporting physicians, 7, 8
lebensunwerten lebens, 48
lethal drug injection, 23–25, 72–73, 84–86, 91, 97
Libanius, 30
life, prolonging, 8, 17, 23, 46, **54**, 55–56, 58
life support, 14–15, 22–23, 70, 88, 95
  laws governing, 49, 61, 93
  living will and, 23, 61
  modern medical technology, 53, 58, 59, 61, 63, **71**
"life unworthy of life," 48

living will, 22, 23, 61, 62, 63
London, Jack, 49
Lucretius, 34

Mannix, Kevin, **83**
martyrdom, 35–37, 41, 43
Masada, 35–36
mass suicide, 36
Medicare, 60
Meier, Diane E., 107
mental health, 37, 40, 63–64,
    81, 104
mental retardation, 49, 50
Mercitron, 73
mercy killing, 29, 45, 46, 50, 79
Middle Ages, 37, 43
Minois, Georges, 39, 43
minors, 14
misinformation, 103
Missouri Department of Health,
    67
modern medicine, 51, **71**
    experience of dying and,
        52–53
    prolonging life, 8, 23,
        51–53
Montaigne, Michel de, 40, 41
moral philosophy, 42–43
More, Thomas, 38–39
morphine, 44, 55, 78
Morse, Robert, 58, 59
motorized wheelchair, 12, 13
Munk, William, 44
murder, 23, 37, 72–75, 78, 94,
    103
    self-, 35–37, 43, 64
    state-sanctioned, **31**

narcotics, 44, 53
National Right to Life
    Committee, 82
Nazi atrocities, **47**, 48, 49, 50
Nero, 35
Netherlands, The, 78–81, 95,
    105
*New England Journal of
    Medicine*, 46, 80
New Jersey Supreme Court, 59
Nitschke, Philip, 97
non-voluntary euthanasia, 23,
    81, 103
Not Dead Yet, 88, **89**
nursing homes, 62, 69, 104

O'Connor, Sandra Day, 88
old age, 32, 34, 35
ombudsmen, 103
Onwuteaka-Philipsen, Bregje,
    81
Operation Rescue, 69
Oregon Death with Dignity Act
    (DWDA), 25–27, 82–85,
    83, 91–93, 96, 103,
    105
Oregon Department of Human
    Services, 84
organ donation, 62

pain, 16–17, 20, 23, 29
    euthanasia to relieve, 35,
        38–39, 44–46
    management, 85, 86,
        106–107
    medication for, 24, 44–45,
        53, 56, 84, 99,
        106–107
    palliative care and, 60
    suicide and, 32, 34, 41, 55,
        64, 84, 93
painkillers, 44, 53
    "double effect," 23, 45, 53,
        81
palliative care, 24, 44, 56, 60,
    86, 107
palliative medicine, 107
Parkinson's disease, 93
passive euthanasia, 45, 53, 96
Patient's Bill of Rights, 56

Patient Self-Determination Act (PSDA), 62
patients' rights, 63, 103
persistent vegetative state (PVS), 58, 67, 69, 70, 75
personal liberty, right to, 86, 88
Phaedo, 33
philosophical suicide, 34–35
philosophical views on suicide, 32–35, 40–43
physician aid-in-dying, 24, 78, 80, 91, 96
physician-assisted suicide, 21, 29–30, 46, 72
  defined, 24
  efforts to legalize, 7–8, 77, 82, 85–89, **87**
  international view of, 94–97, **95**
  in Netherlands, 78–81
  in Oregon, 82–85
  pro/con arguments, 100–103, **101**
  public opinion concerning, 90–92
Pius XII, Roman Catholic Pope, 53, **54**
Plato, 33
Postma, Geertruida, 78
pressure sores, 12
privacy, right to, 58–59
proxy, 23, 58, 61, 62, 63
psychological therapy, 73, 80
public opinion polls, 46, 90–92, 104
Pythagoras, 32

quadriplegic, 12, 15
quality of life, 17, 21, 25
Quill, Timothy, 85, 86, **87**
Quinlan, Joe, 58, 59
Quinlan, Julia, 58
Quinlan, Karen Ann, 57–61, 64, 66–67, 70, 75

race, right to die and, 93
Rehnquist, William H., 68
religious beliefs, 56
  Christian faith, 13, 15, 36–41, 97
  Islam, 97
  Judaism, 35, 36, 97
  opinions based on, 97–98, 100
  right to die and, 9, 15, 70, 93
Renaissance, 37
Republic, 33
Republicans, conservative, 93
respirators, 53, 58–59, 61, 63, 86
resuscitation, 22, 53, 62
review boards, 103
Rights of Terminally Ill Act, 96–97
right-to-die, **26**, 50, 59
  debate over, 7–9
  before Supreme Court, 66–70, 75
right-to-die movement, 15, 63–66, 75, 78, 85–86, 104
  internationally, 94–98
right-to-life movement, 66, 69, 82, 84, 94, 97
right to refuse treatment, 17–18, 49, 55, 56, 58-59, 68, 86, 88
Roe v. Wade 58
Roman Catholic Church, 36–37, 39, 53, **54**, 58, 70, 93, 96–97
Romans, 30, 33–35, 36, 37
Rosenfeld, Barry, 78
Russell, Bertrand, 46

sacredness of life, 100
Saint Christopher, 56, 59
Sander, Hermann, 50
Saunders, Cicely, 56
Scandinavia, 96
Schiavo, Michael, 69

Schiavo, Terri, 69, 70, 75
Sefer Hasidim, 35
"self-deliverance," 64
self-murder, 35–37, 43, 64
Seneca, 34, 35
Shaw, George Bernard, 46
slippery slope metaphor,
   104–105
Smith, Gordon, **83**
Smith, Wesley J., 107
social issues, 7, 19, 37–39, 42,
   75, 107–108
Socrates, death of, 31, **31**, 33, 64
The Sopranos, **57**
Souter, David, 89
South Africa, 94
Sparta city-state, 30
state-ordered suicide, **31**, 33
Stoics, 32, 33
suicide, 13, 55, 63, 99–100.
   See also Physician-assisted
   suicide.
  alternative to, 60
  in ancient world, 30–36
  assisted, 8–9, 15, 18, 38,
    50, 53, 60, 63, **65**, 72,
    75
  assisted, disabled and, **11**,
    13, 15, 88, 89,
    104–105
  assisted, in Netherlands,
    78–81
  assisted, in Oregon, 82–85
  assisted, international
    approach to, 94–98
  assisted, pro/con debate,
    100–108
  assisted, Supreme Court
    view, 85–89, **87**,
    93–94
  as culturally honorable, 29,
    33–34
  as decriminalized, 63, 75
  emotional, 64

  how-to manual, 66
  "justifiable," 65
  kinds of, 64–65
  morality and, 42–43
  philosophical, 34–35
  punishment for crime of,
    30, 40, 42–43
  rational, 64, 65
  as sin against God, 35, 36,
    53
suicide laws, 30, 40, 42–43
Svart, Lovelle, 25–28, **26**
Switzerland, 95

Tada, Joni Eareckson, 10, **11**,
   12–15
Tada, Ken, 13
taedium vitae, 34
terminally ill, 23, 29, 44–46, 61,
   73, 80, 86, 105, 106
  active voluntary
    euthanasia, 64–66, **65**,
    77, 79, 96, 104
  assisted suicide and, 90–92,
    93
  defined, 24
  hospice and, 56, 59, 60
  suicide and, 24, 25, 63, 64
Thanatron, 72
Thebes city-state, 30
Time magazine, 50
trends in dying, 55–57

Uhlmann, Michael M., 39
United Kingdom, 63, 94
U.S. Congress, 62, 75
U.S. Constitution, 68, 88
  Fourteenth Amendment, 86
U.S. Supreme Court, 58, **65**,
   66–70, 75, 83, 84, 85–89,
   87, 93–94
Utopia, 38–39

Vacco v. *Quill*, 85, 86, **89**

value of life, 107–108
ventilators, mechanical, **71**
vocabulary of special terms,
　22–24
Voltaire, 41, 43
voluntary euthanasia, 8–9,
　14–15, 23, 29, 38, 40, 46,
　50, 60, 64, 72, 74, 77, 79,
　80–81, 93–94, 104

Washington v. Glucksberg, 86
watchdog groups, 103

Weiner, Sandra, 99
Wells, H. G., 46, **47**
Wertenbaker, Charles, 55
Wertenbaker, Lael, 55
white race, 93
Williams, Samuel D., 45
Wolf, Susan, 94
women, as at risk, 94
Woodman, Sue, 19, 20, 21
World War II, **47**, 49

Youk, Thomas, 73, 74

About the Author

Rebecca Stefoff is the author of many nonfiction books for young adults, including *Marriage* and *Security v. Privacy* in the Open for Debate series. In addition to books on history, exploration, nature, and science, she has authored works on social history, writing about topics such as environmental activism and legislation, immigration, and American-Indian rights. Stefoff makes her home in Portland, Oregon. Information about her books for young people can be found at www.rebeccastefoff.com.